Camille Oster – Author
www.camilleoster.com
http://www.facebook.com/pages/Camille-Oster/489718877729579
camille.osternz@gmail.com
@camille_oster

The Cursed Bride

By Camille Oster

Chapter 1

Black Forest, German Confederation, 1865

AS THE COUNTRYSIDE PASSED by outside the carriage, Heinrich held Aldine's hand. His hand was large and course compared to her own, and she studied the differences between them. It was still hard to imagine that this beautiful man was her husband. Blond and strong, with an open face, strong nose and pleasing jaw. Everything about him seemed lovely, and he had been very gentle with her throughout their honeymoon by one of the beautiful lakes just north of Milan.

Having grown up so close to Italian lands, Heinrich spoke Italian easily and had been able to speak to all and sundry during their honeymoon. Throughout, he'd shown he was easygoing and struck up conversations gladly.

Looking out the window, she surveyed the landscape outside, the darkening woods that were to be her new home. The Black Forest. Heinrich had assured her it was the most wonderful place in the world. Forests that sang in the breeze and magical landscapes that drove the imagination. To Aldine, it looked scary. She wouldn't like to get lost here.

This was not the area she was from, having been born and raised north of here. But the winters were tolerable and the summers wonderful, she had been assured.

His family was awaiting their return. She had only met them briefly just after the wedding. His mother had looked very regal, and his brother handsome. They were a handsome family, and Heinrich was the master of the estate called Schwarzfeld.

Even the name was a little gloomy, but Heinrich's love for his home was obvious, so she had great hope she would be happy there.

All marriages had some trouble, her mother had told her, and not to be disheartened if not everything was perfect. A husband and wife had to learn to suit each other. So far, they suited well.

The gold band on her finger glinted in the pale sunlight, which came and went with the trees they passed by. Tall pines blocked out most of the sunshine, but intermittently, they passed idyllic villages along mountain valleys.

"Now we are close," he said, regripping his hold on her hand.

Aldine's eyes searched out the window for her new home. The Graven family was old, their history here going back centuries, or so both Heinrich and her father had told her. It was a brilliant match for her. She had married well. Very well.

Heinrich was smiling, pleased to be returning home. "You will like it. You will see," he said. Pulling his hand away, he straightened the arms of his jacket. It had been a long journey through dramatic landscapes, but slowly and steadily they had progressed.

Finally, the house came into view—built of grey stone. Three stories with a turret, and a pitched, slate roof. A very stately house. Ivy grew along the front of it. It was at least two hundred years old, if not older, with both some baroque and gothic features. It had been redesigned at some point in the past, it seemed. Probably around a hundred years ago, if she were to guess. Undeniably a handsome house.

"What do you think?" Heinrich asked.

"It is very stately. A fine mansion."

With a nod, he seemed to approve of her assessment.

The carriage pulled up along the main entrance, gravel crunching under the wheels before stopping. Heinrich jumped out and held his hand for her to take, while someone was coming out of the house to greet them. Firstly, what looked like an elderly retainer.

"Weber," Heinrich said, addressing the elderly man. "I hope all is well here."

"Of course," Weber said. "Your mother and your brother are both at home."

The woman Aldine recognized appeared through the door. Heinrich's mother. Dressed in elegant dark green silk which rustled when she walked. "Heinrich. You return," she said to her son. "I trust the journey went well."

"We encountered no problems on the road. The carriage took the journey well."

"It has been a while since it's endured such a long journey. You must tell us all about it. And here is your bride," the woman said, taking Aldine's hands and holding them out as if surveying her. "As lovely as the day you wed. Please, come inside, Aldine, see your new home."

Heinrich's mother walked ahead of them. Aldine didn't know her name yet. The introductions had been swift. At least Aldine hoped so, or she had forgotten her mother-in-law's Christian name.

With his hand extended, Heinrich urged her to go ahead, entering a large hall with a grand staircase made of rich mahogany. She wondered if it was as old as the house, her eyes gazing over the ornate wood carvings that accented the corners of the staircase that skirted every side of the hall.

Taking Heinrich's arm, she let herself be led into a salon, where the brother, Ludwig, was sitting with his wife. Ludwig smiled as they appeared. "Home safe and sound," he said and rose to greet them. Ludwig put more attention into his clothes, Aldine noticed, the sumptuous clothes reflecting the height of fashion. Perhaps Ludwig spent more time in cities than Heinrich did.

While well dressed, Heinrich didn't seem to pay particular attention to fashion. He certainly hadn't during their two weeks in Italy. He had, however, bought a nice saddle that would arrive in a month or so.

It had been interesting getting to know this man who was now her husband, seeing how he interacted with the world and the people around them. There seemed to be a real affection between him and his family too, which was comforting to see. It would be awful to have to navigate a bitter and feuding family, but all seemed well here. The two brothers appeared close.

"You all remember my wife, Aldine," Heinrich said.

"We do remember. It was merely two weeks ago that you wed," Ludwig's wife said. If they had been properly introduced, Aldine couldn't remember. It had been such a harried and rushed day; she had paid so little attention to everything except where she was supposed to be and what she was supposed to say. Little else had sunk in. Her parents had been there—proud of the match they had achieved for her. Her younger brother too, who had probably preferred to not be there at all.

It was still strange to imagine she would see her family so seldom now. These people in the room with her were her new family. These were the people she would see day in and day out, and they were all strangers to her—even Heinrich, in most regards.

Ludwig's wife stretched for her hands and Aldine wished she knew her name. She seemed very nice. Aldine held great hope they would be friends. "You must be exhausted. Come sit. Would you like a coffee, or perhaps a tea? It is still some hours until supper."

"Or perhaps you wish to rest?" Heinrich's mother suggested. "Your room has been prepared for you."

"Why bother? So recently married, I doubt she will spend much time in there," the brother said quietly and his mother slapped him on the arm.

"Pay him no heed. He is a rude, uncouth creature," the older woman said, lifting her hand to the retainer, who seemingly knew exactly what she wanted. "Weber will bring a fresh pot. Sit."

Aldine did as directed. It was a fine room. Green silk on the walls, and a richly carved fireplace, in the same style as the stairway in the main hall.

"I must go see to some things," Heinrich said, and Aldine felt a moment of panic as he left her alone with his family. It would likely not occur to him that it would make her uncomfortable, or perhaps he should not be tending to her in their own home. Aldine smiled at the people now taking their seats around her.

"How was your honeymoon?" the brother's wife asked.

"It was lovely. Such a beautiful place," Aldine said. "Please, you must all call me Aldine." The Graven title was still a shock to her, and she wasn't used to it. Plus, these people were now her family.

"And you must call me Elke," the brother's wife said.

Aldine smiled, now having a name. The same was not offered from Heinrich's mother, and Aldine would continue with the formal dowager Graven title.

A steaming pot of coffee was placed down and Aldine smiled, sure it would revive her somewhat after the long journey.

"We know so little about you," Elke continued, pouring the coffee to whoever indicated they wanted some.

Aldine felt the dowager studying her, the stoic expression on her face giving little away. "I come from Manheim, where I grew up."

"Your father is renowned for his architectural talents, I believe."

Her father had been celebrated for his work around the growing city of Manheim and nearby Stuttgart. Her grandfather was the third son of a fine family in the district, so they were still considered gentry, albeit removed from the heights of society. Little inherited wealth was coming their way, but her father earned respectable commissions from his architectural assignments. "Yes," she said. "He is currently working on the designs for a guild building in Stuttgart. I'm afraid I don't know the details of it." Of late, her father hadn't often shared the details of his work, primarily because her mother had felt Aldine's attention needed to be on her upcoming nuptials.

With coffee dispensed to everyone, the conversation continued around which buildings they admired in the nearby towns, most of which Aldine didn't know.

Chapter 2

THE ROOM THAT HAD been given her was beautiful. Rose-colored silks decorated the walls, while the furniture was finely carved wood, much like the rest of the house. The window overlooked a lawn with the trees of the forest beyond. The gravel outside the main entrance was in sight too.

Beyond, from what she understood, there were fields that belonged to the estate, but she could not see them—only trees. Heinrich had promised to show her the estate in the afternoon, but this morning he had to see to the business of the estate.

Anna, the maid she had been assigned, was pinning her hair and Aldine sat patiently until she finished. The girl was shy and said very little, avoiding Aldine's eyes whenever she looked at her through the mirror.

It was raining gently outside, little spears of water forming on the leaded window panes. Purposefully, she forced herself not to think about what her parents and brother were doing that day, or that it felt a little as though she had been severed from her family.

But it would do no good to think such. Now she had a husband and things were as they always would be. There would be no going back to the life she had known.

The maid was done and Aldine rose, ready to leave her room, hoping she wouldn't get lost. A hallway led her to the main staircase. It was a beautifully appointed house with portraits of previous generations on the walls. Even swords from bygone eras.

She didn't have long to explore, because Weber found her and led her to the dining room where Elke was eating breakfast. An array of cold meats and cheese lay on the table, and she picked to suit herself.

"I think it will rain today," Elke said. "Sometimes it doesn't stop, but a forest does need rain. It won't be too heavy, though."

"Heinrich said he would show me the estate in the afternoon."

"That should be nice. Do you ride?"

"Not well."

"Raised in the city. There are some nice families around, but one must travel."

"Is your family from nearby?"

"Not far away," Elke said, leaning back and placing her napkin beside her. "It can feel very isolating here, with all the trees, but you will soon meet the people nearby. It is not like living in the city, though, I would imagine. People around here have known each other for generations."

It was hard for Aldine to grasp such a concept.

"The post only goes once a week, though, if you have correspondence to send. I imagine you want to tell your family you've arrived safe and sound."

"Of course," Aldine said.

"If you like to walk, there is plenty of walking, but don't get lost. Fortunately, there aren't so many bears and wolves anymore, but the boars can be dangerous. They will gore you and do horrific damage."

Listening intently, Aldine stopped chewing. Heinrich hadn't mentioned anything about boars.

"And they're fast. They can come out of the forest, charging with their long, sharp tusks." Elke used her fingers to accentuate around her mouth.

"Are they truly such a danger?"

"Only if you're unlucky," Elke said with a smile. "I had one charge my horse once. That's why it is much better to ride. Horses can strike them with their hooves."

In fact, Aldine was a little scared of horses, being so large and unpredictable. Now she had to be scared without a horse as well. This she hadn't realized. The forest surrounding the house seemed much more ominous.

"You find all sorts of things in the forest. Old, deserted cottages. The forest has a long history. There are a few mills as well, sawing the lumber that is harvested. And mines. It has been known to happen, people falling into old mineshafts. But look, I am scaring you. It is not my intention. Only to warn you. It is safe to stay on established paths, but wandering around the forest should be left to those who know the area well. Both Heinrich and Ludwig do know this land like the backs of their hands. If they say it's safe, it is. As boys, they ran all over this forest."

As would her children, Aldine realized. They would grow up here and face the perils of boars and mineshafts. It was still hard to imagine that there would be children. Would she make a good mother? She hadn't even worked out how to be a good wife yet.

Saying something about flowers, Elke got up and left. She did smell a little like flowers. Obviously a perfume she wore. It was lovely, but Aldine also preferred spicier perfumes that made her think of distant lands and exotic places. Scent had a way of carrying one away. But then there was a fresh scent here. Even within the house, there was the scent of pines. Forests smelled fresh without the coal and fires of the city. Even so, a fire crackled in the grate behind her.

Finishing her breakfast, the search for the scent of the forest drove her outside. The doorway had a covered stoop and she stood there watching. It was so quiet, except for birds. No people, no carriages, no distant whistle of a locomotive—just thick, pressing silence. It was simply that she wasn't used to it. It was as though she was in the middle of a sea of wilderness out here. That probably wasn't remotely correct, it just felt that way for a moment.

Pulling herself together, she pushed such sentiment away and looked around. The air was fresh and wet, with the scent of rain. The gravel road leading from the house was where they had come yesterday. From the journey, she knew the estate was quite high in the mountains, but it didn't seem it just here.

With her step away from the entrance, gravel shifted under her feet and she walked ahead to look back on the building, which stood large and solid behind her. Ages of family history were encased in this house, and she was now a part of it.

Off to the side were buildings, which she assumed were for farming purposes and probably a stable. The carriage would have a house too. It was too fine to leave to the ravages of weather.

Where was Heinrich? Off somewhere. There was no sound to indicate anyone was outside, until she heard hooves coming closer.

Turning, she looked, but saw nothing. Searching the trees, she sought a glimpse, eventually seeing flashes of a horse cantering. The sound grew louder as the horse and rider struck the gravel. He wore a hat and a coat.

Aldine smiled. Heinrich was home a little earlier than she'd expected—he'd said afternoon, but here he was.

As she watched, though, his features became more clear, shifting from what she knew. This wasn't Heinrich—instead someone else. It was easy to see how she could have assumed so, because they looked alike. This man was darker, though. Not quite as golden, not quite as fine in features—

more masculine. That wasn't right. Heinrich was a very masculine man, but this man was... harder.

"Who're you?" he said, reining the horse in. A blatant statement without much finesse. This man didn't have the look of a servant. His clothes were well-made.

"I am Aldine... Graven."

"Heinrich's new wife," he said, but it was a statement more than a question. Smoothly he dismounted and pulled the reins over the horse's head. The man turned to assess her, and Aldine didn't know where to put her hands. Who was this man?

"Enchanted, I'm sure," she said when the man didn't introduce himself.

It spurred him into action. "Wolfgang. Half-brother. Neither part of the family, nor not."

The frown must have spelled her confusion. There was another brother? She didn't remember hearing of him.

"I am the illegitimate son of the former Count Graven." There was a bitterness in the statement. He didn't seem to hide it. "I live in one of the cottages. Not the house." And clearly he hadn't been invited to the wedding, but he had known about it.

"Oh, I see," Aldine said, unsure what to say.

"I take it Heinrich didn't mention me."

No one had mentioned him. It was as though he wasn't there.

"He has spoken more about the land than the people. I still don't know his mother's name," she confessed.

The man smiled as he undid the straps of the horse's girth. "Wilhelmina. I have other names for her, but I won't share them."

Taking the saddle off, he carried it over one arm as he led the horse away and around the corner of the house without saying anything more.

Well, that was curious. There was another brother, who seemed to be acknowledged enough to live on the estate, but not enough to be considered family.

"There you are," she heard from the doorway. "What are you doing outside? It's raining. Come inside," Elke said. "I will show you the house. I'm sure Heinrich forgot to."

"I just met the other brother, Wolfgang."

"He's back, is he? Yes, well, come inside. No point standing out in the rain."

It was barely raining, more like a mist of wetness. Turning to the door, Aldine attempted to smile. Being a stranger in a strange house felt a little claustrophobic. She felt in the way and awkward, not knowing the routines and traditions of the house and family. It was something she would learn, this awkwardness a necessary period that had to be suffered through with as much grace as she would manage.

Chapter 3

THE RAIN HAD STOPPED in the afternoon when Aldine and Heinrich headed out in the open carriage. The air was fresh and there was even gentle sunshine. Heinrich held the reins and drove, a very competent driver. It pleased her, all the things he could do. He wasn't one of the city men who depended on others to do all things.

Looking at his profile, she again wondered that this man was her husband. A handsome, titled man with a thriving estate. How had she been so lucky? Handsome, considerate and kind. It was almost as if she didn't deserve such happiness.

The roads were narrow, but well-kept. In places the land was rugged and stony, thick moss covering everything. Forest so thick, it seemed impenetrable. In other places, it was lighter in tone with ash trees and birches.

Emerging at a plateau, the landscape opened up, forests of pine beneath them, a dark lake, and snow-capped mountains in the distance.

"It is so beautiful," Aldine said.

"Yes. Honestly, I get so caught up in everyday life, I don't always notice."

Driving further, they came to a village with large, sloping roofs, built entirely of timbre. A few people milled around the village, a few raising their hats in greeting to Heinrich, who returned the gesture.

"Is this village affiliated with the estate?" she asked.

"Partially. Most work with lumber, some with dairy."

They passed a stone church with a thin, sharp spire. It was not the church they had married in, which seemed to have been a larger one in a town nearby. She wasn't sure exactly where that town was. She and her family had stayed at a nearby inn while getting ready, and set off on the honeymoon right after the quick reception held at the town hall.

"I met your brother," she said as they left the village. "Your other brother, I mean."

"Wolfgang?" he asked.

"Yes, he came riding." Perhaps she should not mention that he had been rude—not deliberately rude, more lacking in manners. It wasn't as though it had offended her; she had simply noted that he didn't prescribe to the manners that Heinrich and Ludwig did.

"He lives in one of the cottages," Heinrich said. "I wasn't aware he has returned."

Aldine found it difficult to ask what role he had in the estate. Being illegitimate as he was, it could be a sensitive topic. "Should we expect him for supper tonight?"

Beside her, Heinrich seemed to shrug. "Usually not. He only tends to appear on special occasions, but I suppose a new bride does qualify, so he might. He is always welcome, of course." Was there a bit of strain in his voice? Odd that he would rarely dine with them if he was welcome. How families treated illegitimate children differed from family to family, but it did say something that he lived on the estate.

"You do look alike," she continued. "I thought it was you riding up for a moment. I suppose partially because he wore a hat."

"He takes after our father. We both do, I suppose."

They headed into a very wooded area again, the landscape darkening considerably. A building was hidden amongst the trees, almost as if it emerged from the rocky landscape behind it, the brick being discolored to blend into the forest. Attached to it was a large wheel being turned by the stream coming down the hill, and a chimney bellowed smoke.

"The mill," he said. "This is where the lumber is sawn."

"You spend time here?"

"Yes, so does Wolfgang. He deals more with the sales, which is why he often leaves."

"But not Ludwig?"

"Ludwig is more suited to dealing with the estate accounts."

Continuing on, they drove through forest that got denser and denser, almost blocking all light.

"Elke told me there are boars," she said.

"Yes," he smiled. "We hunt them when we can."

"I understand they are dangerous."

"They can be, particularly during rearing season. Mothers defending their young. It is always the female of the species that is most dangerous, I find. But outside of rearing season, it is not much to worry about."

"Elke said it is perilous to walk in the forest."

"If you are loud and they hear you coming, then they pose no threat. Elke is overexaggerating."

"She was just trying to warn me," Aldine said, feeling as if she needed to defend Elke's intentions. "With my background, I am not used to forests. She also mentioned mineshafts."

"Now that is true. Mostly, those we know of have been labeled, but further away, they can pose a danger as the growth covers them. It is always a good idea to tell someone that you are walking and in which direction."

With a smile Aldine nodded, not sure who she should believe, Elke or Heinrich. Perhaps Heinrich's familiarity with the place made him blind to the perils. Then again, if she believed Elke, she would be marooned in the house for the rest of her life. Getting to know the perils and learning to deal with them was a much better option.

They emerged to a field that looked somewhat familiar. Cows grazed lazily in the mild sunshine and the road skirted around the field.

"Thank you for showing me the estate," she said, taking his arm and placing her head on his shoulder. "I still struggle to fathom that this is where I am to live, and that you are my husband. We shall be happy here, won't we?"

It took a moment before he smiled and she noted the hesitation, but didn't understand why it was there. "I hope so," he said calmly. "I hope we will be very happy." With his hand, he stroked hers wrapped around his other arm.

A mile or so and they were returning to the house, coming from a direction she hadn't come from before.

Taking her by the waist, Heinrich lifted her down from the carriage. "Do not be afraid to walk nearby. It is quite safe. It's not rearing season for a while yet, and even then, if you make some noise, a sow will not bother you. Even just a little humming. They have good hearing."

"Alright," she said, feeling assured. There were a great many things she felt assured about when he had her in his arms.

"Now, there are a few things I must do before I retire for the day." Leaning down, he kissed her and Aldine received it with affection. The honeymoon was over and he had to return to his duties, but she wasn't sure she was ready for it to be. It had been lovely and sweet getting to know each other during their time in Italy. Here he seemed to be gone most days.

Getting in the carriage again, he took his seat. "Too much bother to unharness and simply ride. I won't be long." He winked before he drove off and Aldine watched him go.

It had been a lovely afternoon, but she could use a refreshment, still a bit sorry that he couldn't stay with her. That was something she would have to get used to. He would be back for supper and then they had some hours to while away after.

"There you are," said Wilhelmina, today again looking regal in her stately and somber dress, which she seemed to prefer. "I was just about to have some coffee. Would you like a cup?"

"I would," Aldine said, thinking it would do well to dispel some of the chill from the afternoon ride. "Heinrich has just shown me the estate. It's very large."

"Yes," Wilhelmina said, leading the way to the salon, where in a corner by a window, she sat. This had to be where she took afternoon refreshments, Aldine assumed.

"Very beautiful landscape."

Weber arrived with a beautiful porcelain service, pouring hot, steaming coffee into two cups. "Sugar?" he asked and Aldine shook her head. She liked the bitterness of it.

"I liked the way the Italians drink their coffee. Thick and dark."

"Perhaps you should have a bit of milk—in case there is a child growing," Wilhelmina stated.

"I don't like it with milk."

"When it comes to family, what we like is of secondary importance, is it not?" With that, she poured a measure of milk into Aldine's coffee. Smiling, she returned the small milk jug. "We have excellent milk here. The best in the country, I would say."

"Yes, of course," Aldine said, smiling tightly as she received her cup.

"We are all so looking forward to having small feet running around the house again."

It was natural that she should want grandchildren, Aldine concluded. Obviously, it was on the woman's mind. Ludwig's marriage had not produced any as of yet, and

Wilhelmina was turning her attention to the new union, it seemed.

Blowing on the hot liquid, Aldine took a sip, encountering the creaminess of the milk. She really did prefer her coffee without it. Perhaps she'd had better get used to coffee this way until she produced the heir the family needed. It was the point of this union, after all. It would be a stretch to say it was a love match, but the union had been proposed, and Heinrich had been courteous and considerate at every meeting she'd had with him prior to the bargain being struck. Both herself and her parents had concluded he was a man she could fall in love with over time, and she had seen nothing in him since that would suggest otherwise.

Chapter 4

HER HEART WAS BEATING out of her chest, and waking felt like a rush from a chaotic dream world to the stillness of the real one. Darkness surrounded her, but her heart still beat wildly, making her feel like she needed to fight her way out of the blankets. There was no danger, no threat, but her dream had been horrid. She couldn't remember what it had been about, but it had been bad. Heinrich had been there.

Turning, she saw him gently sleeping beside her. Sleeping soundly, he always looked so peaceful. Bare shoulders. Was the room warm? It wasn't to her, but then her nightgown had an uncomfortable stickiness. The horrid dream had made her perspire.

Sitting up, she peeled it over her head and placed it on the floor. It made the blankets feel a little better and she snuggled closer to Heinrich's warmth. Now that was a lovely feeling, when he put his arm around her as they slept.

The marriage bed was lovely too. It had been worrisome and distressing at the very start, her being unsure what to do. No one had explained it, and it wasn't something you spoke about, as such, with your husband, was it? Now, though, she felt she had an understanding of what it was about, and the intimacy was shifting from awkward to comforting.

Her heart finally calming, she closed her eyes again, but the effects of her dream were still on her mind, if not her body.

Nightmares were not something she usually suffered from. Her mind was usually too calm for such things.

Obviously there had been nightmares when her grandmother had died, but that was to be expected. There was nothing now to cause her such concern, but perhaps taking on her new life here at Schwartzfeld was more overwhelming to her than she realized.

Leaning over, she kissed Heinrich on the cheek. It was strange to think she had a husband to kiss now. Her parents' relationship was quietly affectionate. They never gave themselves to wrought emotion, and neither did she. So this nightmare was unusual.

No, it was too hot to sleep next to Heinrich and she shifted away to a cooler part of the bed. Still, sleep eluded her as she closed her eyes.

There was an inherent problem with having someone in her bed—she couldn't simply light a candle and read, so she lay there, staring at the ceiling. The headboard was ornate above her, oak leaves and acorns if she recalled right. It looked like nothing more than shadows right now.

Some night bird squawked outside and Aldine slowly rose out of bed and softly walked to the window. The moon was full that night, so she could see the lawn outside, painting everything in ghostly moonlight. Nothing moved, until she saw a fox running across the lawn.

It was so much cooler over by the window. Her skin was starting to contract with the iciness. The fire had died in the grate, nothing but cold ashes.

She had no idea what time it was, if it was close to dawn or even past midnight.

Wrapping her arms around her, she stood for a while longer, until the cold grew intolerable. Then she returned to the bed. Funnily, she seemed to get warmer the closer she got to the bed. Perhaps it emanated.

Stepping back, she felt the shift from warm to cold wash over her almost like cold water being added to a bath.

How curious. Perhaps it was how currents worked in the room. Houses could be like that, the design creating air currents. If built wrong, wind could positively howl down corridors. These were things a good architect knew. Longing for home hit her suddenly and fiercely. It was hard to believe she would never live with her parents again, the only home she had ever known.

Shifting beneath the blankets, she lay down again. It really was warm. Placing her hand on Heinrich's shoulders, she felt his heat. Definitely warm. Not clammy like fever, but warm. Perhaps he was simply warm and the space around him warmed.

On the wall behind the bed was a painting. In the dark, it looked little more than scribbles, but she knew it was a painting of people from the village. She hadn't looked at it too closely, had only noticed people sitting and standing around in a room.

Closing her eyes, she pretended to sleep, until it finally claimed her.

Next, she woke with a start, sunshine beaming in through the windows. The bed shifted and she startled even more, but it was simply Heinrich putting a knee on the bed so he could kiss her. "I must go," he said, his lips seeking hers. Tilting her head back, she received the kiss. Kissing was nice. She liked kissing.

He was dressed, putting on his jacket over a soft linen shirt. Dark boots covered his feet and ankles—perhaps practical in a forest.

"Sleep some more," he said and Aldine smiled as she watched him walk out of the bedroom and close the door.

In truth, she felt horrid. Drained and tired, but she couldn't fall asleep again. The sun was a little too bright, perhaps. It was much brighter than the previous day. Likely, she would dare to venture out on such a day. It would be warm and clear.

Rising, she felt the tiredness in her body. It must be the nightmare that had drained her so, or the fact that it had taken her so long to fall back asleep. With her blankets off, she remembered that she was completely nude, and the room was cold. With Heinrich gone, so was the heat of having him in the bed. She shivered as she quickly pulled on her nightdress, before darting into her own room, which was just as cold when she bathed and dressed in a new shift.

With a ring of the bell, Anna appeared to dress her hair. The girl had brown hair under a large mobcap. "Is your family from here?" Aldine asked after the girl silently went about her task.

"From the village," she said, her accent a little different from Heinrich's.

"It's nice that you have a position so close to your family." Aldine smiled tightly, again feeling the distance to her own family.

The girl nodded and brushed Aldine's hair. As a well-trained domestic servant, she only spoke when spoken to.

"I suppose you walk to the village," Aldine continued.

"Yes."

Others walked around comfortably, and so would she. The fears that had built in her were unreasonable and she had to overcome them. Today, she would walk outside, along one of the established paths, so she didn't by chance fall down some discarded mineshaft.

Finally done, she made her way downstairs, where both her sister and mother-in-law were sitting at the dining room table. It seemed all were early risers here, but then they didn't have terribly late nights either.

"Good morning," Wilhelmina said. "I hope you slept well."

There was no point bringing up her lack of sleep, so she simply smiled as she sat down. "It seems to be a beautiful day. I am going to venture out for a walk."

"Would you like me to join you?" Elke asked.

"Wonderful idea," Wilhelmina added. "You should go together. Show Aldine the paths around the house. Tomorrow, we must go to service in the village. Our church is much smaller than the one you are used to, I am sure."

"The family built it," Elke added.

"I saw the church," Aldine mentioned. "Heinrich didn't say that the family was responsible for its construction. It looks old."

Putting her cup down, Wilhelmina looked at Aldine. "Built in the year 1550. The stone was quarried nearby, I understand."

"I am curious to see what it looks like inside."

"It seems you have inherited your father's curiosity for buildings."

"Well, it was a topic discussed every day, so perhaps I could not fail to take an interest."

"Such a modern girl, aren't you?" Wilhelmina said.

Twisting her head slightly, Aldine tried to figure out what the statement meant. Was it a compliment or an insult? Wilhelmina's face wasn't giving her intentions away. "I simply am as I was raised to be."

"Of course," the woman said with a smile. "Aren't we all?"

Placing her napkin down, Wilhelmina rose, her skirts rustling as she moved out of the dining room.

Elke made an exaggerated grimace for a second. "She disapproves of everything modern. Beyond rearing children and comforting a husband, she sees no role for women outside the home."

Intellectual development was a noble pursuit in Aldine's family. "I suppose she won't approve of attending lectures, then?"

"Well, you can try if you can find one. Not too many lectures around here."

"I will have to make do with the library," Aldine said with a smile.

"If you like animal husbandry and agricultural practices, then you are in luck. The family bible makes interesting reading." The wryness in her voice was humorous, and Aldine thought they could be good friends. They were a little isolated out here in the mountains of the Black Forest, so it would be wonderful if they could be friends.

Chapter 5

STANDING IN THE GRAND hallway, Aldine waited for Elke to come down ahead of their walk. Punctuality did not seem her greatest trait. As far as Aldine could see, Elke did nothing in a hurry. Perhaps there was no need to hurry here. The days were long and there wasn't much to keep time to, other than luncheon and then supper.

Shifting her foot slightly, Aldine noticed the red carpet she stood on. It was old, but of good quality. Quality always lasted. The dark red gave a dark quality to the room, which was already somber from the wooden paneling on the walls. The window did what it could to brighten the place.

Portraits were staring down at her and she studied them. Handsome, strong faces, with the serious expressions that were the fashion of previous eras. Men in black clothes with white lace collars. Who wasn't pleased fashions had changed? It was only the clergy that kept such morose and somber clothes now.

One man had long hair and a sharp, piercing gaze that seemed to look straight at her no matter where she stood. Still handsome, but there was a harshness about him that the artist had captured.

Looking closer at some of the other paintings, they were village scenes, again with the somber clothing. People gathered in a town hall, or something similar. A pastor at the pulpit, leading the congregation. There were definitely religious overtones to many of the pictures. It suggested it formed a great part of the family history.

"The Graven family is very old," Elke said, drawing Aldine out of her study. "Extensively tied to the Lutheran church. Even faithful supporters of Martin Luther himself, I believe. Apparently not enough to give up the family title completely."

That she was Lutheran had been imperative in the marriage contract, so it was still important to the family, even if Heinrich didn't act like an overly devout man, other than a quick prayer before supper.

The sun was warm as they walked outside, and the sky blue. It was warm enough to walk with little more than a shawl.

"The weather can change very quickly. The clouds rolling in across the forest, plunging the whole area into fog. It's really cloud, I think. We live in the clouds here at times."

"Hopefully the weather won't come in while we're out."

Elke walked them to a path that led into the forest. The thick canopies blocked out much of the sun and it instantly felt colder. A carpet of green moss covered the whole of the forest floor, looking like a raucous sea over slopes, rocks and boulders, even felled trees. "In the early autumn, the forest fills with blueberries. It's wonderful. And then mushrooms, all different kinds. Although you have to know which ones to pick, some are poisonous. I am sure there is a book on them in the library. It is very important to know which mushrooms to pick and which to avoid."

They walked arm in arm down the path, reaching a small bridge over a ravine. Again, the whole of it was covered by moss, almost making it all look soft. "It is such wild country," Aldine said.

"In places. Other places it is gentle with rolling hills. Heinrich showed you the dairy fields, did he not?"

"Yes," Aldine said, still appreciating him taking the time to show her his lands and industries.

In the distance, they saw a cart traveling along the road. Again she thought it was Heinrich for a moment, before seeing it was Wolfgang.

"Wretched man," Elke said. "Why doesn't he just leave?" Then she caught herself and smiled. "He can be very quarrelsome. He's a thorn in the family's side."

Aldine didn't know what to say. "Does he have family elsewhere?"

"None that will have him."

Although Heinrich had expected it, Wolfgang hadn't appeared for supper the previous night. "He is not married, I take it."

"Well, who would have him? He has nothing. Doesn't stop the dairymaids from clambering after him. I'm sure he toys where he shouldn't."

The bitterness in Elke's voice showed clearly she disliked the man. As did Wilhelmina, apparently, according to Wolfgang's own inference. Heinrich seemed more welcoming, although Aldine hadn't heard Ludwig say one way or the other.

It had to be awful to be in that position, part of a family where at least half of it wanted not a bar of him, wishing he would simply go away. It was perhaps understandable that he was rude and bitter.

"Come, let's return to the house," Elke said, throwing a last dirty look at the man who hadn't noticed them before he disappeared from view.

*

The church was freezing inside when they entered through the main doorway. Grey stone covered all of the floor, with a carved stone window above the altar. Small windows high along the walls let in some light, so it was a bright space, albeit cold.

Dark wooden pews lined the sides and they took their seat at the very front, which Aldine assumed was for the family. A simple wooden cross hung on the wall, but there wasn't much adornment otherwise, except for the carved pulpit.

The pastor was a middle-aged man who wore a black robe over his black cassock. It made him look pale, but he had a kind, round face.

With long strides, he walked over with his hand outstretched. "Welcome, Countess Graven. I am so pleased to meet you and welcome you to the congregation."

"Thank you," Aldine said.

"I understand you are from Manheim. Deacon Walter, I presume."

"Yes," Aldine said, pleased and impressed that there was a connection between her own church and her new one. This seemed to go well. So far, she liked her new pastor, hoping they would get on well. Some in the Lutheran church were a little fervent.

The sermon started shortly after she sat down next to Heinrich, enjoying the warmth of him next to her. They were to have the day together and Aldine was looking forward to it. His hand took hers, his fingers entwined. Sometimes he was very affectionate, and other times, he seemed to want to keep her at a distance. It had confused her at first, but now she simply accepted his intermittent affection.

Her hand was small in his, his skin calloused and rough. Those hands had traveled her body that morning, elicited urgent desire that seemed to grow stronger each time they lay together. It was a base act, but it had its own beauty, she had concluded. It was growing on her. But now was not the time to think of such things.

The pastor was talking about tolerance and of when to be firm, but Aldine found it difficult to concentrate. There was so much curiosity about her new family. Even Wolfgang was there, but he was sitting in the pew behind them. It seemed in church, he wasn't fully part of the family. Tolerance didn't fully extend to him, it seemed. Or perhaps, she was the one taking his place, displacing him out of the family to be forced to sit in the pew behind.

Quickly, she looked behind her to see him looking down into his lap. They looked so alike, him and Heinrich, yet one was the titled progeny and the other the illegitimate scourge on the family—according to some. It seemed unfair.

The sermon was over and they rose to sing a hymn, then another. Then it was over and they could return to the warmer temperatures outside. If it wasn't for Heinrich sitting next to her, she would really have frozen. She knew for next time to dress warmly.

"Pastor Stubbe," Wilhemnia said with apparent affection when they reached the doorway, where the man was farewelling his congregation. "It was a lovely sermon."

"Yes," the man agreed. "We all have our duties to perform and we must do so to the greatest of our abilities, even if it is hard."

Aldine wondered if the man was referring to Wolfgang. Perhaps not, but the sermon surely applied to her illegitimate stepson. So far, though, she had barely seen Wilhelmina acknowledge his presence.

"It was such a pleasure to have you with us," Pastor Stubbe said, taking Aldine's hand.

"Yes. And a riveting sermon," Aldine replied. It might not have been riveting exactly, but it had been good. The virtues were difficult to enact uniformly in one's life, but she tried to be mindful of her own impact on the world.

"Of course, any instruction you would wish, I would be happy to help."

"I will keep that in mind." Pastors often seemed to expect that they went home and studied the bible after service. Perhaps the Graven family did. It remained to be seen what they did with the rest of their Sundays.

Walking arm in arm with Heinrich, Aldine greeted the sun and let it warm her face. Wilhelmina was speaking to a contemporary and even Elke had found someone to chat with. Aldine knew no one here but the family. Wolfgang didn't loiter and was already on his horse, riding away.

"Excuse me, I must speak to someone," Heinrich said. "Won't be long."

Her hand slipping out of his arm, she let him go. This was the one place the whole community met and mingled, so it wasn't a wonder everyone liked to mill. Normally she would be having a word with her friends too. Instead, she looked around. It was a lovely church. Narrow, but very pretty.

Around her was the graveyard, and her eyes soon found a Graven. The date said it was only recent, but there had been no mention of this person. A sister?

"Come," Heinrich said, drawing her attention away. "Let's head back for some luncheon. I am starving. Pastor Stubbe is coming to join us."

"Oh, that's wonderful." In fact, it was the first time they'd had a visitor of any kind.

Chapter 6

TAKING HEINRICH'S HAND, Aldine stepped into the carriage and was followed by both her mother and sister-in-law. Heinrich and Ludwig took their seats on the driver's bench and they were quickly on their way back to the house.

That grave she had seen still lingered on Aldine's mind. She'd never heard mention of a Josefina, who had died only last year. There were no indications of this person by anyone, or any signs of her in the house. Still, it didn't seem suitable to ask when everyone was present, in case it was a very sensitive topic, which it seemed to be if all reminders of her had been cleared away.

It wasn't a long ride back to the house, no sight of Wolfgang when they got there. Pastor Stubbe was not far behind in his own plain carriage, and they received him in the salon. Mr. Weber retrieved drinks for everyone, including an elderflower cordial for the ladies.

Pastor Stubbe was speaking to Wilhelmina about an upcoming event within the village, while Heinrich and Ludwig spoke about some machine that had been introduced at an agricultural fair.

None of the conversations included her, and that suited her fine. There was little she could add to either. Elke was shifting her skirt to display it better.

"Who was Josefina?" Aldine asked quietly.

"Where did you hear that name?" she asked.

"I saw her grave."

"Ah. Well, she died. We don't talk about it. It's hurtful. Please don't bring it up."

"I'm sorry," Aldine said, feeling admonished.

"The past is best left there, at times. More cordial?"

Her glass was still three-quarters full. "No, I'm fine." It was a bit sweet for her liking.

"Would you prefer some tea? I like a bit of mint tea before eating. I find it prepares my digestion. Shall I make some? I think I will. Won't be long." Rising, Elke disappeared and Aldine was left to observe the company again. Both Heinrich and Ludwig were relaxed, having moved to the fireplace to smoke.

"Do you play any instruments?" Pastor Stubbe asked Aldine.

"Not well. We were never much of a musical family, I'm afraid."

"That is a shame. Music is such a delight for the soul."

"I do enjoy going to concerts," Aldine added. "When they're on," she drifted off under Wilhelmina's harsh scrutiny.

"Not much in terms of concerts around these parts," Wilhelmina added. "We must make our own music. Perhaps you should practice."

With a tight smile, Aldine nodded.

"Here we are," Elke said, returning with two cups in her hands, placing one down in front of Aldine. "There is more if you would like," she said to her mother-in-law, "but you are not a fan of mint, are you?"

Without responding, Wilhelmina turned her attention back to the pastor, who was now talking about what appeared to be another lady living in the district, and her two young sons, who were just about to go away for their schooling. Apparently the woman lamented being without them.

"It is always difficult when your sons go away, but they do come back. Unlike daughters. But we are then blessed with daughters-in-law."

"And such lovely additions to the family," Stubbe added. He seemed genuine in his compliments. There was an openness about him that Aldine liked.

"Where did you attend seminary?" Aldine asked.

"Munich," he replied. "It is where I am from originally."

"You must miss it," Elke said.

"At times. The Black Forest is such a beautiful place, such rugged beauty, one cannot help but to be swept away by the romance of the landscape."

"You have such a way with words, Mr. Stubbe," Wilhelmina said and the pastor's cheeks colored slightly. "Poetic."

"Do you write?" Aldine asked.

"I dabbled a little in my youth, I suppose, before I became immersed in my work after."

Weber arrived to tell them that luncheon was ready to be served and they shifted to the dining room. Heinrich sitting at the head of the table, while it took a moment for Aldine to realize that she was supposed to sit on the other side. Normally Wilhelmina headed the other side of the table, but not today. Not in front of company, it appeared, where Aldine had to take her rightful place as the mistress of the house.

Feeling a little awkward at this elevated status, she sat down. It would be far worse to argue. She actually preferred sitting next to Heinrich, but he was still in full view.

A large trout had been placed at the center of the table, covered with green herbs and onions. It looked delicious and smelled wonderfully. A maid served the portions out, starting with Heinrich, and then hers, followed by the guest. The dining process was much more formal when they had company. It reminded her of when she had dined with her father at the Academy of Architecture, where they had been served with gilded cutlery. It had been a very fine affair and Aldine had worn a gown specifically commissioned for the event.

As luncheon finished, Elke decided to retreat upstairs to her room to rest, but the rest of them went outside to see the pastor off just as Wolfgang was returning from wherever he had been.

"You missed lunch," Heinrich said to his half-brother.

"Needed to be elsewhere," he said as he dismounted.

"There is plenty left over if you should wish," Ludwig called back as he walked inside.

Wolfgang nodded, proceeding to take off the saddle and bridle. His horse didn't move when free to do so, even walked behind Wolfgang as he carried the saddle to the stables' tack room. The horse seemed to trust his owner implicitly, probably expecting a feed of oats. Aldine didn't actually know what time horses ate.

"How are you, my dear?" Heinrich asked. "Did you enjoy our lunch?"

"It was a lovely meal."

"I believe Ludwig caught the trout this morning."

"He did a splendid job." Stepping a bit closer, she wanted to touch him, for him to put his arm around her perhaps. Maybe even kiss her, but he didn't. "What do we do now?"

"Whatever you wish," he said. "Read. We can play cards if you like. I know Elke really likes cards."

The idea was appealing; she wanted to spend time with him. It felt as though she had barely seen him all week. They did share a bed in the evenings, but there wasn't much talking between them. Other than that, they had very little time together, and it seemed they wouldn't have much now either.

"What is it? You looked concerned," he asked.

"Not concerned as such. It's just that I saw a grave in the graveyard."

"There are many graves in the graveyard."

"Josefina Graven."

The easy smile melted off his lips for a moment, but he covered the expression. "She was part of the family for a while, but she died. It was very sad. No reason to concern yourself. The past is the past." His sentiment on the topic seemed to echo Elke's. Taking her hand, he tugged gently on her arm. "We will play cards. I'll just refresh for a moment and I will see you in the salon."

Stepping back, his fingers slipped out of hers before he turned and walked in the door. Aldine stood there, trying to understand what he'd just said. Part of the family for a while. What did that mean?

Crunching steps sounded and Wolfgang walked around the corner. There was something uncomfortable about his presence, and she didn't know how she was supposed to deal with him, choosing to smile.

"Josefina was Heinrich's bride before you," Wolfgang stated and Aldine's mouth opened in surprise.

"I didn't know," she said quietly.

"She died and now they don't speak of her."

"Did he love her?" It seemed a crucially important question and she voiced it before she had time to think about it.

Wolfgang raised his eyebrows as if the question surprised him. "Not sure they knew each other long enough, but who can tell? I suppose only Heinrich would know that."

Except Heinrich clearly didn't want to speak about it.

"And Luise before that." Wolfgang added.

"Luise?"

"Heinrich has had a string of bad luck when it comes to brides. Some around here say he's cursed, but they're a superstitious lot. Any slight coincidence and it's a curse. The exact same people who believe in moss folk, goblins and elves. No rational person would put any stock in it."

Cursed? Of course she didn't believe in curses. Beliefs from centuries before. "Moss people?" she said. Well, there was certainly enough moss around.

Two brides lost. Aldine had had no idea.

Wolfgang walked into the house, which was the first time she had seen him enter the house. Was he to while away the afternoon with the family, or did he simply wish a belated lunch?

For a while, Aldine stood staring after him. Heinrich had lost two brides, Josefina and Luise. This had never been mentioned. Not that either she or her father would have put any stock in any notion like a curse. Perhaps his reticence to spend time with her was a result of this. How close had he been to them? Had his heart been broken, not just once, but twice? Or had he not known them well enough to have developed deep feelings for her, them?

Aldine didn't know what to make of this news. In a way, she felt sorry for Heinrich for the loss he had endured, but she was also here because of this loss. A negotiated bride he had barely known. Was that not the same for the other two? Had one of them been someone he'd known for a long time, one he'd been in love with? Elke had said it was hurtful to talk about it.

Absently, she stroked her fingers across her lips, unsure how to feel about this new information, or even if she was better off knowing this. She could have chosen not to ask. Heinrich had chosen not to tell her, but Wolfgang had obviously overheard the question and answered it in his stead.

Suddenly this marriage seemed much more complicated. There were other people in it—ghosts.

Chapter 7

"THERE YOU ARE," Heinrich said as Aldine rejoined them in the salon. "Elke is not down yet. Perhaps we should wait for her."

Wilhelmina was sitting in one of the chairs, reading, while Ludwig lay reposed on a sofa, looking bored. Wolfgang, for being in here somewhere, was absent. Perhaps he had gone out the kitchen door at the back.

"After she can play a little music for us. She plays so beautifully."

In some ways, Aldine should feel inadequate as a bride for not being able to play the piano well, but she was too distracted by the news she had just learned.

Forgoing the cards table, Heinrich sat down in another chair and accepted a glass of wine from Weber.

"A recuperative?" he asked her as she stood there, not quite sure what to do with herself. All week she had been praying for Sunday to come around, but now that it was here, she didn't know what to do, almost wishing she was alone.

Two brides lost, she repeated to herself. That was unfortunate. Perhaps that explained why he came all the way to Manheim to find a wife. If people around here really were superstitious, they wouldn't promise their daughters to him. The kind of bride a man in his position would seek, though, would likely not be of the superstitious sort.

Heinrich wasn't looking at her, instead looking out the window. His handsome face had belonged to other women—for however brief a time. It appeared not to be long if Wolfgang was to be believed. How could he say something like that and simply walk off? More worrying was perhaps how unforthcoming Heinrich had been on the issue. Perhaps he saw it as none of her business. In a way, it was none of her business as these things had all occurred before their marriage, but it still felt like something she should know.

Wilhelmina looked up with a smile. Was she disappointed with the caliber of the latest bride, the third choice? "Sit down, girl. No point standing around like a shadow."

"Of course," Aldine said, blushing as she took the nearest seat. Sitting was not what she wanted to do, so she rose again. "I might pick some flowers. It's such a nice day. I could use some subjects to draw."

No one argued as she walked out of the room and she paused by the doorway, feeling a sense of panic. What if she never settled with her husband? What if she was never comfortable here?

Questions were bouncing around her head. Had he been in love with one of these women? Did he mourn them? Where did that place her?

Fresh air seemed to calm her slightly and she walked over to the edge of the lawn where wildflowers grew just at the start of the forest. Crouching down, she picked a few flowers. They were perhaps not of any sort that had scent, but she could use them as models for her drawing. She'd always liked drawing flowers.

A small crack drew her attention up and into the dark forest. Nothing was seen, but something had cracked in there, followed by a thick silence until the wind rustled leaves above her.

Moss people—what a silly notion. Although it wasn't a stretch to imagine creatures in a forest, was it? Of course she didn't believe such things, but a forest was alive with creatures large and small. The quiet eeriness of it almost convinced you that all sorts of things could live in a forest. It was almost as if you looked long enough, something would show itself.

Picking the flowers she wanted, she hurriedly returned to the house, preferring the distraction of her drawing book to the tingling weariness she felt when she stared into the dark forest-scape. Quickly retrieving her drawing case, she picked out the lead pencil she wanted. Once finished, she could water color it.

It had actually been a while since she'd drawn like this, but right now, she felt like she needed something familiar to distract her from the thoughts circling around her head endlessly.

*

After a somber afternoon, where Aldine immersed herself in her drawing as much as possible, it came time to rest before supper, when she retreated to her own room and savored the chance to spend time in her own company.

The Heinrich she had known in Italy seemed more and more distant to her. She felt no closer to him than she did any of the other people in the house, and that was troublesome to her. In some important way, he'd withdrawn from her.

Nights were still spent in his bed, but that intimacy had a purpose, one that Wilhelmina seemed intent on reminding her of regularly.

Truthfully, she didn't feel like dressing that evening and wondered if she could say she was unwell, but that might have Wilhelmina up here, worrying about the health of their investment. If she could only go home. It was her most fervent wish right at that moment, but she couldn't. She could never go home again. She belonged to the Graven family now, and only an act of the most depraved abuse would justify her returning to her family—and that included from her parents' perspective.

By no stretch of the imagination was Heinrich abusing her. He was very cordial and considerate, constantly asking if she was cold or if she needed anything. His manners could not be faulted.

A small knock on the door signified that Anna was there to smooth and re-pin her hair. Aldine smiled weakly as the young girl walked in. She seemed a nice girl, shy. The only person Aldine spoke to who wasn't part of the family, not that Anna appeared all that willing to speak.

The girl quietly moved into the room and closed the door, before carefully unpinning Aldine's hair. "I heard today of moss people," Aldine said. "Such superstitions are not common where I am from."

"I wouldn't think there was much moss in cities."

"No, I suppose not," Aldine said with an amused smile. "Such beliefs are common here?"

"Some hold to the old ways, even in this age," she said.

"You believe in such things?"

Anna didn't answer for a while. "The forest has a life of its own, and its own secrets to keep. You don't live here without discovering that. It's its own being."

"Are you scared of it?" Because the truth was that Aldine was. There was something very uncomfortable about the alien darkness of its nooks and crannies, hidden from the sun and everyone else.

"No need to be scared of a forest," Anna said as if it was a ridiculous question. "But things pray on people's minds around here, always have. In the olden days, they feared witches used the spirits of the forest to do their bidding."

Aldine didn't quite know how to accept the statement—whether to be astounded more at there being witches or the forest spirits that did their bidding.

"Not so much, these days," Anna said. "But I suppose you are right that it is good to be wary of the forest. It holds many dangers, and things can happen and you won't be found for months. People have been known to disappear."

"Were you here when the count was married before?"

"Before my time," Anna said. "I've only been here a few months."

"Oh, I see."

"But you know about them?"

Anna looked increasingly uncomfortable, probably picking up that she was being interrogated. "Best you speak to the master about them."

It wasn't the answer Aldine had wished for. "Yes, of course," she said, turning her gaze back to herself. Witches and spirits. This part of the world certainly had an interesting history. At times, it seemed the modern world took a long time to reach here, being hidden away as everything was. It was a place that kept secrets, it seemed—both this house and the forest that surrounded it.

"Thank you," Aldine said when Anna was finished and slipped out of the room as quietly as she'd come in. It was growing dark outside, the shadows merging together as one, pale blue light silhouetting the tops of the trees. The sun had already gone down, this was just the last light of the day.

Reaching for a match, Aldine lit the candle that stood on her dressing table. There were proper lamps, but she was leaving in a few moments to go downstairs for supper. Perhaps she was extending this moment by herself a little longer than she should. It was time to learn what a Sunday supper was like in this house. She could always hope it was the calm, languid affair it was back home, but she felt anything but languid in this family—tense was perhaps the right word, but maybe every bride felt that way when they were settling into their husband's family. It was simply a process to go through, like every married woman before— even Wilhelmina. Although it was difficult to think Wilhelmina was ever uncomfortable and foreign in this house. The house and the family seemed synonymous with her.

Chapter 8

"YOU HAVE BEEN SO QUIET," Elke said as they sat down for afternoon tea the following day. "I made us some mint tea. I've been having problems with my digestion lately."

"Thank you," Aldine said, accepting the cup. It smelled fresh, but was sweet with sugar.

"I hope everything is alright," Elke continued after taking a sip of her teacup.

"Yes, of course." It wasn't perhaps completely true. These two previous brides were on Aldine's mind. She'd tried to bring it up again with Heinrich the previous night, but he had quickly shut down the conversation, making it clear that he didn't want to talk about it. "I suppose I can't help but be curious about what happened to Josefina."

Elke stared at her for a moment. "She grew ill and died," she finally said. "It was very tragic. Barely married. Please don't bring it up. There is nothing to be gained. Heinrich has suffered the most atrocious ill luck."

Placing her cup down, Elke rose and strode across the room, signifying she would not speak more about it further, but it didn't satisfy the questions in Aldine's mind. Where was she from? Where were her things? How long had they been married? Had he loved her?

There certainly wasn't an opening to ask about the other bride, Luise.

Wilhelmina entered the salon with a vase of flowers. "The marigolds are blooming. Aren't they beautiful?"

So far, Aldine hadn't seen marigolds blooming anywhere. It didn't seem to be by the house.

With Wilhelmina's attention on her, Aldine smiled tightly. "Yes," she said.

"You really should learn how to arrange flowers," the older woman said.

"I have sufficient knowledge for such things," Aldine replied carefully, not wanting to sound confrontational, but she was the daughter of an architect and arranging flowers was a way she could express those principles. In fact, she'd created much more elaborate flower displays than the one Wilhelmina had just carried in, but then she'd had access to every type of flower the Manheim flower market had. "I can take over some of those duties, if you wish."

Even as Aldine hadn't intended on it being a challenge, the woman took it that way. The tightness of her mouth showed it. Aldine had only been informing her that she had some capabilities related to the topic. Apparently she'd said something wrong. It was hard to know how to deal with this woman, what role she was supposed to play in the house. Had Heinrich's other brides been the same, or was she a disappointment of some kind? It could be that Wilhelmina mourned one of the previous brides as well. Trying to smile, Aldine managed to feel some sympathy to her.

When she'd come here, she hadn't realized this was a house in mourning. Past the mourning period, but that didn't mean much. Mourning didn't happen to the schedules society dictated.

Taking another sip of her mint tea, Aldine withdrew from the interaction. She simply didn't know where she stood with these women—even her husband when it came down to it. Everything had shifted so fiercely since the day she'd arrived.

"I might go for a walk. Are there still marigolds blooming?"

"Yes, they are over by the farmhouse across the eastern field. Weber retrieves them if you ask him. There are dahlias and pansies too."

"Some exercise will do me good." Rising, Aldine went outside. It was still warm enough to walk without a cloak or coat, at least until the late afternoon, or unless the weather changed. The warm hours weren't long in duration, but they were lovely while they lasted.

Going outside, she felt relief from the expectations on her and the fact that she was in some ways failing to meet them, but couldn't exactly pinpoint how. Heinrich was off somewhere. Although titled, he was not a man of leisure. His estate was a going concern and needed to be managed.

The eastern field was through a stretch of forest with a well-established path, covering her with its humid darkness before emerging in a sunny field. The field crop, whatever it was, was green and swaying in the breeze. It was a while from harvest, she guessed as she walked around the edge of the field to the farmhouse.

As she got closer, she could see neat rows of flowers being grown specifically for the Graven household. Sprinkles of color dotted across the rows, and Aldine smiled seeing them. She could come here to draw, sit here in the sun and draw real, live flowers. They had a very different vibrancy to them than they did when cut and dying. Today, she hadn't even considered bringing her pencils and watercolors.

Turning, she saw the wind dance across the field. It really was beautiful in the way only nature could manage. A simple majesty.

But then dark thoughts broke into her mind again, capturing her as if to drag her down into doubt and uncertainty. She had been better off not knowing about the other wives. Perhaps Heinrich had been right in not telling her. This information had brought nothing but darkness and doubt into her thoughts.

A distant noise broke into the peaceful scene before her, and a horse appeared. Wolfgang. She was getting better at telling them apart. He was cantering along the edge of the field on the far side, not seeing her or giving indication that he saw her. His horse veered into the path returning to the house, or rather his cottage.

Running her hand across her mouth, she considered him for a moment. He seemed to be the only one telling her about these brides, although she wasn't entirely sure of his motive for doing so. It wasn't as if he held any loyalty to her, but perhaps he simply felt she should know.

Hurrying around the field, she followed him back to the house. He might be long gone by the time she got there, being substantially slower on foot than he was on horseback, but she found him in the stable, pouring oats into his horse's trough. Taking care of his horse was something he did personally, it seemed.

Looking up as she entered the stable, he stared at her blankly. There was never a welcoming smile with him, and she wouldn't hazard a guess if he remotely liked her. Not that they knew each other, but he did seem the most willing to talk. That could be a guess, just because he had mentioned the brides to her in the first place.

The truth was that she needed to know. Half knowing made everything much worse. Now that she knew of them, she needed to know the whole truth, while everyone else was happy never to mention it. But they all knew what had happened—she'd only had a few hints, and it was preying on her mind.

"I understand Josefina died of sickness," she said.

Wolfgang didn't answer and picked up a pail of water and placed it inside the stall. "You should talk to your husband."

"He doesn't discuss it, and my mind is running away with half-truths."

"Do you suffer with a mind that runs away with fantastical notions?"

"I simply wish to know what happened and no one is telling me."

"They are very good at not telling," he said cryptically. "They're very good at lying too."

"What is that supposed to mean?" Aldine stepped further into the stable, so she could better see his face. Little of what he said made sense to her, as if he was speaking in riddles.

"Nothing," he finally said. "Yes, Heinrich's second bride grew ill and died."

"Did he love her?"

"How am I supposed to know? Not the kind of man who makes declarations of love in front of all and sundry. You'll have to ask him."

"And the other?"

Wolfgang pursed his lips for a while. "Slipped and fell. Hit her head. It killed her."

"In the house?"

"In the forest."

Somehow, that answer felt worse. Notions of moss people and sprites whirred through her head, before she controlled her own ridiculous thoughts. Wolfgang would likely ridicule her if he knew what actually crept up in her mind. If his brother was not one for public declarations of love, Wolfgang didn't seem one for kindness and understanding. There appeared to be a very hard core to this man, but at least he was answering her questions.

"Who found her?" he asked.

"Heinrich. We all had to go search for her when she didn't come home. We found her the next day."

"She must have gone far."

The man shrugged and picked something from his pocket and put it in his mouth. "Not too far. We simply didn't find her until the next day."

"That's awful." Elke's warning to be careful in the forest made more sense now. Aldine supposed there was little point in asking if Heinrich loved her either. "Was she from around here?"

"Not far away." So they had likely known each other growing up. Wolfgang was running out of patience with her and pressed past as he walked out of the stables, leaving her to her own thoughts.

Aldine supposed that all she really wanted to know was if Heinrich's heart was closed to her, and she still had no more information on that count. Poor Heinrich, losing two brides. It had to affect him, but she had seen no trace of that sorrow in the man she had grown to know during their honeymoon in Italy. Had he not known these women enough to mourn them deeply, or had the man she had gotten to know been a lie?

Chapter 9

STARING OUT AT THE PASSING landscape, Aldine tugged slightly on her glove. They were visiting a friend of Wilhelmina and it was the first time Aldine was to be introduced properly to what society there was around these parts. It was something that was expected and Aldine liked that they were doing very normal things after the upset and concern she'd had.

For a few days, things seemed calmer. Aldine felt as if she did know the basics of why Heinrich was a widower twice over. One bride had grown ill and died, the other had fallen and hit her head. Both very unfortunate events, and neither of them particularly questionable. It was simply bad luck it happened to Heinrich's brides. Both seemingly within months of marrying him.

It was perhaps understandable why superstitious people would assign meaning where there simply wasn't any. Poor Heinrich, how much he'd had to bear. It was also understandable that he was a little remote perhaps, but he was kind and considerate.

"Lady Thainer is married to my second cousin Walter," Wilhelmina said. "She will be curious to meet you."

Aldine had to purposefully suppress the question in her mind if she had been equally as curious about Heinrich's other brides. It did not help with her mind running away with such things. She needed to stop thinking this way.

They turned into a smaller road, which led them to a house that looked a little more Italian in design, large and rendered with pale stucco, windows lining the front façade in neat rows. It was very different from the local architecture, but then the gentry tended to choose their architectural style from a broader selection. It was beautiful.

"Welcome," a woman said as they stopped in front of the house. Appearing in a silk gown, this could be no one other than Lady Thainer, Aldine guessed as the woman came down and embraced Wilhelmina. "It is a delight that you could come see me today, and your lovely daughters-in-law." The woman's attention turned to Aldine. "And such a beautiful girl you are," she said and Aldine blushed at the barefaced compliment. "Please come in, have some refreshment with me. Mrs. Muller has baked this morning. She does wonderful pastry."

It was warm as they walked inside. A fire had been lit, even as it was a relatively sunny day. The parlor was also in a more Italianate design. Lady Thainer was seemingly a fan of the southern aesthetics.

"Walter isn't here, and he will be sorry to have missed you. I hope all is well with your family?"

"Of course," Wilhelmina said. "The boys are always busy."

"Such hardworking men. I understand why you are so proud of your two boys. Please come sit, Countess Graven," she said, patting a chair next to where she herself sat down, and Wilhelmina stared at Aldine until she recognized this referred to her.

Doing as she was told, Aldine sat down and Wilhelmina took the other chair, but there was none for Elke.

"Oh, we must find a chair for you, of course, Elke. How remiss. Herman, please bring a chair for Elke. Quick, man. He is so slow. It's such a trial when your retainers age. Walter won't hear of us letting him go, even as I tell him, we must let the poor man retire."

Herman came carrying a chair and placed it on Aldine's other side. The table already had a silver coffee pot and four cups lined up. Luckily, whoever prepared the coffee didn't forget Elke was coming.

"Are you well read?" Lady Thainer asked.

"I suppose. I like to read."

"I am so enamored with the Greeks and the classics. It is a treat to meet people who share my passion."

Elke fidgeted with her skirt and it drew Lady Thainer's disapproval, so Elke stopped.

"Your father is Mr. Richter, the architect, I believe."

"Yes," Aldine said.

"I have seen some of his work. Marvelous. You must be very proud." Pride seemed to be central to this woman's view on life, Aldine concluded.

"Yes, of course."

"Perhaps he can help us a little. We are trying to build a new spire for the church over in Freibronn. We are raising money to build a new one. The old is in complete disrepair, it is beyond saving. It was struck by lightning, would you believe? Weakened it substantially."

"I can ask if you wish."

"That would be wonderful," she said with a smile. "A spire of some acclaim then. Wouldn't that be fortuitous?"

Wilhelmina and Lady Thainer went on to discuss some of the notable members of society nearby until it was time to leave.

"It's a shame my daughter wasn't here. You should meet some of the young people in the district, of course, but she is in Stuttgart just now. We must meet again when she is back."

"That would be lovely," Aldine agreed.

"Now you must go before the weather turns. Herman assures me it will. Feels it in his knee."

56

As they walked outside to their waiting carriage, Lady Thainer waved to them from the top of the stairs as they embarked.

There was silence in the carriage as they pulled away, Wilhelmina seemingly lost in thought, as was Elke, who had mostly been ignored by the hostess throughout this visit. Either Lady Thainer didn't like her or she was a stickler for hierarchy and treated Elke as a mere wife of the second son. This made Aldine question the woman's kindness—if it was simply afforded to her because of her position as a countess in the region. Some people were like that, deferred to title and status more than the person carrying them. It was not how Aldine liked to see the world, preferring to think of people on their merit. Now it made her wonder if Lady Thainer's interest in her father had been simply to point out her more humbler roots, and that the shift from an architect's daughter to a countess was notable and deserved remark— even if veiled.

Oh how she hated that she questioned everything, but perhaps this was all normal. Unfortunately, she didn't have anyone to ask. Her relationship with Wilhelmina and Elke did not extend to such frank revelation of her own insecurities, and she suspected that would continue.

"That wretched boy," Wilhelmina said harshly, breaking into Aldine's musings. For a moment, she had no idea what Wilhelmina was referring to until she saw Wolfgang in the distance.

"What's he doing now?" Elke asked.

"Always skulking about," Wilhelmina said, her lips in a terse line. "Always hangs around and covets what's not his. Heinrich refuses to tell him to leave. He is too soft that way, completely remiss to the fact that the softness is not returned. Jealous and resentful, ever since he was a child. I never trusted him around the boys. Never. When can we ever be rid of that wretched man, who hangs around like a shadow all the time."

Aldine hadn't realized that Wilhelmina's dislike for Wolfgang ran quite so deep. It was perhaps understandable that Wolfgang didn't spend time with the family. Elke didn't like him either. Granted, he was not the most charming man. In fact, he had few manners at all, but Aldine hadn't seen him skulking around.

"His mother was a mere whore," Wilhelmina continued. "Thought she'd get her claws into a title, stupid thing. Men are too soft with their ill-begotten byblows."

Turning her face away from where Wolfgang was riding in the distance, Wilhelmina's head was high and her spine straight.

In a way, Aldine felt sorry for Wolfgang for having so much dislike directed at him. It could not have been easy for him to grow up in the household with such a resentful stepmother. Aldine assumed Wilhelmina hadn't accept him as a stepchild, just some unwanted bastard foisted on her. His father, though, had accepted him and taken him into the family. Wolfgang wasn't, after all, responsible for how he came into the world, or whatever intentions his mother had had.

The expression on Elke's face wasn't quite as harsh. She was amused and she looked over pointedly at Aldine, then away again. Perhaps she had been privy to this bile directed at Wolfgang before. Was Elke's dislike of him simply a reflection of Wilhelmina's?

As soon as they arrived home, Wilhelmina helped down and walked into the house. Weber then helped the two sisters-in-law left behind.

"Bitter to the core when it comes to Wolfgang," Elke said. "Because if the old count had been given the choice, Wolfgang would be the count now."

Aldine's eyes widened. This was news to her. "He would have married that woman?"

"Marguerite, yes. He was in love with her, it is said, but he would have been disowned if he'd married her. So Wolfgang came to be, but the marriage did not, and everyone knows it, including Wolfgang. It is the true source of Wilhelmina's hatred. Plus also, Wolfgang is a contemptible man. He really is. Jealous and falsely prideful. Only Heinrich cannot see him for what he is. Unfortunately, Wilhelmina can't convince him to send his bastard brother packing. He really should. Be it on his own head."

Chapter 10

SLEEP DIDN'T COME that night. The bedroom felt hot. Heinrich had no trouble, however, and slept soundly. It was too dark for her to see him, but she felt comforted by his slow and steady breathing. Still, she could not get cool and found herself forever turning, seeking a cool spot in the bed.

It had been an eventful day, visiting Lady Thainer, and then the revelations about Wolfgang. It wasn't perhaps surprising that the former Count Graven had been threatened with being disowned for falling in love with the wrong girl. Such things did matter in many families, particularly old ones.

Yet Aldine herself was not entirely from the best circles—respectable, but not titled. It was curious that their marriage had been proposed. But even in the best circles, Count Graven's bad luck with brides probably met a degree of concern as well.

Her mind was so very tired, but her body refused to let her slip off to sleep. A squawk of a bird sounded outside, but the whole house was silent. If only she could sleep. There was nothing to be enjoyed from lying in bed at night, being exhausted but unable to sleep.

*

There was hot air all around her as she walked through the house with lumbering and slow steps. It was indeterminable whether it was light or dark outside. It was dark inside, hidden corners draped in shadows.

She didn't know where she was—or where Heinrich was. He was supposed to protect her.

Her vision shimmered with the heat and the smell of smoke tickled in her nose. There was fire, but she couldn't see it. Not in front or in back, but she felt hot winds lick along her skin, lift strands of her hair.

It felt as though the whole house was watching her. It didn't want her there, and it was hiding itself. From room to room, she walked, but she got nowhere. Old furniture, old paintings, and they moved. People spoke to each other with silent mouths, playing out the scenes they depicted. They didn't see her, those little figures.

The carpet undulated under her feet as if it would lift and fly like a magic carpet, but it never quite pulled away from the floor. She tried to step off it, but the heat got worse closer to the walls.

"Heinrich?" she called, but got no answer. "Where are you?" She had to find him; had to find any of the others. They were in the house, but she couldn't reach them. "Heinrich, I'm scared."

On and on, she walked, going from one room to the next, unable to see out the windows, until she reached one where the shudders were open. There was nothing but clouds directly outside the window. It was dark, but light bounced off the clouds—reds, oranges and yellows. The fire was outside. It wasn't inside at all. It reflected off the clouds almost as if she could reach out and touch them, but it was so hot inside. Was the house burning? Was that where the heat came from?

Aldine started to run, but the carpet seemed to move under her feet in the wrong direction, forbidding her from reaching where she wanted to go. A door to escape—that is what she needed. If the house was on fire, she needed to get out. Everyone else had gone, she realized. They had fled the danger and they had forgotten her, or hadn't found her.

"Heinrich!" she called even louder, but there was no noise. And then there was. The distant murmur of voices. People had gathered outside, watching as the house burnt. But she was still inside, and she couldn't get out. Why wasn't anyone trying to help her?

The carpet was refusing to let her get anywhere, but she knew that if she stopped and let the carpet carry her in the direction it wanted, things would go very badly for her. She had to fight or it would be all over.

Suddenly, it stopped and there was utter stillness. The carpet stopped tugging and stayed still. The heat didn't stop, though. Whispers she couldn't make out murmured around her, but she reached a window where she now saw clearly. They were all standing outside, watching the house. People were gathered from the village, all staring helplessly at the house.

Banging on the window, she tried to draw their attention, but no one looked her way. Heinrich, Wolfgang, Elke, Ludwig and Wilhelmina. They were all there. Ludwig had his arm around Elke, who was crying. Banging harder, she screamed for them to hear her, but no one looked her way.

Tugging on the window, she tried to get it up, because she knew she wouldn't be able to get to a door. If she left this window, she would lose any connection with the outside world and simply be lost in the house again. But the window refused to budge. It would not open for her.

A vase stood not far away, but it would mean having to leave the window and her connection with the world outside, and she wasn't sure it would be there again if she moved away. The vase could smash the window, though. It was her only chance. It was only a short distance away, mere steps, but she feared taking them.

Turning back to the window, she saw them again. A bonfire cast shadows on their faces, but it was the house they were watching. She must break the window. Stepping away, she ran to the vase, but fire flared up the wall in an instance as if it just caught fire. It enveloped the vase. It had been a trap, and she realized it had been.

Every wall was on fire, yellow flames licking up the dark wooden paneling. It was encroaching on her from all sides, crawling along the ceiling over her head. She had to run and she did, but every room she entered was on fire. The varnish on the panels was blistering and cracking, the paintings were starting to burn and flames licked over the door archway she ran through.

She had to find the door out. The kitchen, but she couldn't find it. Salons and parlors were all she passed through, familiar and unfamiliar at the same time.

Her heart beat wildly now as the heat encroached further and further. It licked up her arms, which would blister like the varnish shortly. Her skirt caught fire and she kicked at it in sheer desperation.

Hands took her face. "Wake," he said. Heinrich. For a moment she saw him, then darkness. "Wake," he said again.

Sheets were trapped around her feet and she was desperately trying to free herself.

The nightmare house as had been was gone and she was back in bed, Heinrich still talking to her. "Just a nightmare," he said.

"I was on fire." If her heart had ever beat that fast, she didn't know. Her nightgown was drenched in sweat. "I couldn't get out and you couldn't hear me."

"It's alright. It's over now. Calm yourself." His voice was slow and steady. There was no danger. It had all been a dream. It still took some time to calm her heart and her breath. She'd never had a dream like that before, one eliciting complete panic.

"Shhh," Heinrich said, stroking her head.

Breathing deeply, Aldine tried to calm herself. "I'm sorry."

"It's alright. Everyone has nightmares every once in a while."

Not like this, she said to herself. "Do you?"

"Not for a long time," he said. "But I used to as a boy."

"I dreamt the house was on fire and I was trapped inside. I couldn't get out. The house wouldn't let me leave."

"Dreams are irrational imaginations."

"Yes," she quietly agreed and tucked her hands under her cheek.

"Think of something pleasant," he said, leaning over to kiss her forehead. "Sleep now. The nightmare is done."

The problem was that she was struggling to do so. Her mind was still caught on unpleasant things. This was all simply tension she'd felt recently, she determined, related to not knowing exactly how she belonged here and what her role was. It wasn't perhaps surprising that such a dream should arise, but the sheer panic she had felt was. She'd never been that frightened before. Her body still shook with the tension of it.

With his hand resting on her shoulder, Heinrich fell back asleep and Aldine drew a deep breath. The bed was a mess, she must have kicked the sheets, now she pulled them up again, but the wetness of her nightgown made it clammy and unpleasant. Sitting up quietly, she pulled it off and let it drop on the floor. Too often, she seemed to be doing so recently.

Freezing for a moment, she pulled the covers up her, shuffling herself a little closer to Heinrich's body because the cold wasn't relenting. It was so hard to keep an appropriate temperature in this bed. Most of the time, she was either too hot or too cold to be comfortable.

Holding her blankets in her fists, close to her neck, she breathed deeply again and closed her eyes, praying for pleasant dreams of summer fields, or the flower market back home in Manheim. She loved that market, with all the gloriously colorful flowers, some exotic, like orchids. Tulips and roses. Their petals so soft and almost fleshy, like the dewy cheek of a child. Firmly she tried to recall the smells and the sights that she knew so well.

Chapter 11

LIFTING HER COFFEE CUP to her lips, Aldine drew in the hot, pungent liquid, letting it coat her tongue and warm her as she sat at her dressing table, looking out the window. She felt strangely lethargic today, as if she had just recovered from a fever. It had only been a nightmare, but the tension of it had exhausted her.

Heinrich had already gone, as he did most days, shortly after waking at dawn. He'd kissed her and told her to rest before walking out the door. She'd heard his horse on the gravel below, and him giving orders to Weber.

But it was a pleasant day outside from the look of it. The sun shone and birds chirped. Later, a lovely day for a walk. Stretching her legs might build up some energy in her as well.

Anna appeared at the door. "Are you ready to dress, madam?"

"Yes," Aldine said, but she wasn't sure she was. Part of her wanted to crawl back in bed, but it would only make things worse for sleeping the evening to come.

Pulling one of her day dresses from the wardrobe, Anna laid it out on the bed.

"I think we will keep the hair simple today," Aldine said. It was perhaps a day when she couldn't deal with any level of complexity. The library would serve as a nice, quiet space to read.

Her head tugged slightly with each stroke as Anna brushed her hair. In the mirror, Aldine looked a little pale. Some sun would be good for her cheeks.

"Are you not hungry today?" Anna asked, looking over at Aldine's untouched breakfast that had been brought to her earlier.

"My appetite is missing." Even as she said it, she knew that Anna wondered if she was with child, but Aldine knew it was the previous night that had robbed her of appetite. Although how would she know if she was pregnant? Several days of missing appetite and a queasy stomach, she supposed. Hopefully Anna wouldn't go downstairs and gossip about how the countess was showing signs of childbearing.

Her hair brushed and simply braided, Aldine dressed and put on her shoes, before standing at the door and trying to compose herself. For some reason, she wanted to stay in her room, but that would be unseemly. It was time to face the day and Aldine left, walking down the stairs, to meet Wilhelmina coming out of the salon, carrying a vase of flowers.

"Well, look who's risen. Well past ten. We are not in the habit here of lying in our beds all morning like princesses," she said sharply. "That might be how you behaved at home, but here we live differently." Without giving Aldine a chance to explain, Wilhelmina left the room.

Not quite knowing what to do with such harsh criticism, Aldine just stood where she was. Nothing in her repertoire of appropriate behavior had prepared her for something like this. One did not give credence to false accusations, and one did not talk back to one's mother-in-law. There had been a good reason for why she had risen late that morning, but even in her own head it sounded feeble— rising late because she'd had a nightmare. It was the excuse of a child. It was difficult to explain how this nightmare had affected her, and still did, even now.

Finally choosing to walk into the salon, she found Elke sitting in a chair, reading. Aldine wished her good morning.

"I heard you being a victim of Wilhelmina's foul mood."

"I was feeling a little under the weather," Aldine said, trying to explain her late rising.

"I hope everything is alright?" Elke said, clearly looking worried.

"Just a difficult sleep last night."

"I hate when that happens. When you lie in bed and can't do anything but look at the ceiling."

"Do you have trouble sleeping?"

"Rarely. In the height of summer, when the nights are warm, I suppose. What is giving cause to your trouble?"

In a way, Aldine didn't want to explain how she'd had a nightmare and that her nerves were still frayed. "Just one of those nights," she said, smiling tensely.

Wilhelmina walked back into the room and it felt as though the temperature dropped. Immediately, Aldine felt herself tense.

"We're having the carpets whipped today, so we need to move all the furniture off to clear them. You will both have to help."

"Of course," Elke said with a smile, appearing enthusiastic, which made Aldine appear less so.

"Yes, of course," she added, but knew it appeared a belated afterthought.

"Like I said, we don't sit around like spoilt princesses here," Wilhelmina repeated. "Start in the study."

Putting her book down, Elke gave her a conspiratorial look as she walked out of the room. The study was somewhere Aldine hadn't been, Heinrich's exclusive part of the house. Walking past the window, she saw that whipping structures had been erected outside and maids and manservants had been gathered for the task.

"It's a momentous task," Elke said. "It will take all day."

This was the last thing Aldine wanted, feeling exhausted before even starting such a day, but what could she do? Already she had failed at being enthusiastic enough about this task.

Heinrich's study was dark, the grate cold. Leather-bound books lined the wall and his desk was neat and clear. From what she knew of him, he wasn't one to spend time indoors, bent over accounts. A tray of decanters stood in the corner and above the fireplace was a picture of a severe-looking man, dressed in black, old-fashioned clothes. Clearly looking the way a devout Lutheran did in those days.

"Johannes Graven," Elke pointed out. "Looks like a joyous person, doesn't he?"

The man looked too somber to even know how to laugh. "They were different times, weren't they?"

"They had a lot to lose back then, I suppose. The world was changing, or rather, they were trying to change the world. Especially down here where we have Catholics everywhere we turn."

"The churches were nice in Italy." They had been very different from what she was used to, with gold gilded embellishments, marble statues, paintings of forlorn saints and weeping women. A far cry from the comparatively unadorned churches she had always attended.

"Shush," Elke said, pointing at the portrait. "Don't let him hear that. He'll turn in his grave."

Aldine smiled at the silliness as they proceeded to move a small table and a chair off the carpet that ran underneath. The manservants then came and rolled up the carpet before carrying it out.

*

All day, there had been dust in the air, but Aldine supposed it was a job well done. Carpets did tend to capture all the dust and dirt in the house, releasing it whenever anyone walked over them.

Wilhelmina had gone on to direct them the whole day, and there had barely been a moment to sit down, let alone hide away in the library.

Come suppertime, Aldine was exhausted. If she had any worries about sleeping that night, she was well past that. Every ghoul in the world could come out to haunt that night and she wouldn't notice a thing.

Ludwig had returned earlier than Heinrich, as he often tended to do. He joined Elke on a bench outside for a while, where they talked. Their marriage seemed strong. There was a real camaraderie between them.

Once Heinrich returned, he went upstairs to his room to wash and change.

"Did you not notice the house cleaning we did today?" Wilhelmina asked as they sat down for supper, her taking the head of the table opposite her son, and Aldine sitting next to Heinrich—as she preferred. "Every carpet in the house was dragged out and whipped until they cried for mercy."

"The house does smell a little fresher for it," Ludwig said.

"It was hard work, although it seems city girls are not all that accustomed to work."

Looking up, Aldine looked over at her mother-in-law, trying to understand what she was implying. She'd worked just as hard as anyone else.

"Slumped over the furniture most of the day," Wilhelmina went on, her head held high, but not looking

CAMILLE OSTER

Aldine in the eye, as if she was below regard. Her gaze was on Heinrich.

"Not surprising as Aldine had a difficult night last night. It would have been a hard day for you," he said, turning his attention to her.

"We managed," Aldine said with a smile. "All the carpets were done." In a way, he was standing up for her and she hadn't really expected it. A quick smile lifted the corners of her lips, but then she remembered that Wilhelmina was watching. In whatever power struggle this was, Heinrich had just handed her some power. Aldine wasn't too naïve to know it.

Everyone returned their attention to their soup, but Aldine couldn't help but worry that this would make things worse. A kind word might not be enough to make Wilhelmina retreat, but it meant a great deal to Aldine that her husband stood by her. It gave her hope beyond anything she'd felt since coming here.

Chapter 12

EVERY DAY, IT SEEMED the relationships and personalities within the house were revealing themselves more and more to Aldine. No longer was she the curiosity that Heinrich had brought home and now she had to find her place within the household. Although it seemed Wilhelmina was reticent to give up her role as the mistress of the house, maybe even vying for being the head of the family.

Relationships were complex and she was starting to see that complexity now. It did make them harder to deal with. Ludwig appeared to be the least interested or concerned about her joining the family. Heinrich—well, he was still distant in many ways. She saw more of the women and understood more of the strains between them. In a way, it felt as if she wasn't getting to know Heinrich better than the handsome and carefree man she had gotten to know on her honeymoon. It felt, however, that there was more of himself he wasn't showing her. For example, she still didn't know how he felt about his previous wives. That part of himself, he wasn't letting her see.

Her relationship with Wilhelmina was strained. Perhaps it always had been, but she hadn't seen it before. Nothing she did was ever correct and the older woman went to pains to point out even how she poured coffee incorrectly. Mother-in-laws were notoriously difficult, weren't they? Perhaps this was simply normal. Aldine had never had a mother-in-law before.

Walking was her reprieve and her relief. The paths around the house were lovely once you got used to the eerie silence of the forest. Everywhere she looked, it seemed like a painting, even the darkest recesses of the forest. Nature was wonderful at creating scenes, wasn't it?

This time of year, the air was sufficiently warm to make for a pleasant walk. As with the family, she was starting to notice the details—the birds, the plants, the streams. There were fish in some of them, and they swam like shimmering, silver missiles in the water, scattering as her shadow appeared above them.

Small, old bridges were built over some of them, while others she had to jump across. The water was ice cold. It didn't warm with the weather.

Out here, she felt part of nature, just another creature roaming the forest. It was a feeling she hadn't expected, but as she calmed with her surroundings, she felt comfortable being there. Boulders were warmed by the sun and provided a good place to sit and simply listen. The trees sang with the wind. A perfect symphony—a crescendo whenever the wind picked up.

At first, she had felt safe in the house and at risk outside. Now it was the exact opposite. The forest was never going to judge her or pick on everything she did. It accepted her just as she was.

The path led her on, until she realized that she was not on the path she had expected to be. The surroundings were growing unfamiliar. Tension rose up her spine, but not distressingly. The path would lead her right back to where she had been. Truthfully, she was probably somewhere everyone else knew really well, but she didn't. Had she wandered off Heinrich's land? Unlikely, but she hadn't been paying much attention, simply following the path wherever it led.

The path was the important part. It would eventually lead somewhere she would recognize and she could orientate herself again. Still, she would turn back and retrace her steps.

The longer she walked, though, she wasn't getting to anywhere she recognized. Was she even walking toward the house?

Heinrich knew this land like the back of his hand. He would find her if she got lost. That she knew, but there was still something very uncomfortable about being lost. The comfort of nature around her was now giving her less solace.

The forest was growing denser and more oppressive and the path smaller and smaller. Aldine stopped and didn't know if she should go forward or back. If she turned back, she would be led back to a path she didn't know, and ahead was another path she didn't know. Somehow she had gotten off the safe path onto a new one, and this was not a well-used path at all.

Still, it would lead somewhere and she could not simply stand here in indecision, so she walked on. She simply had to follow the path and not lose it. As long as she was on a path, she was fine.

But this path led somewhere, a ruin, that by the looks of it had been mostly reclaimed by the forest. Overgrown steps led up to a crumbling cottage that was partially built into the root of a large tree. This had not been a fine house even in its heyday. Moss covered everything, but she could see what would have once been a wall. The roof was completely collapsed.

A part of an iron stove stood, the top covered with moss created over layers of decaying leaves. The forest was reclaiming every part of this structure, gently breaking it down and absorbing it back.

Walking up to it, she stepped on the bottom step. Who had lived here? This had to be on Heinrich's land, unless she had walked so far she was off it, but she didn't think so.

The wood gave and she had the uncomfortable feeling of falling before her foot jarred on the earth underneath, a cut ran up her calf and she could feel that she was bleeding. This structure was inherently unsafe, she concluded.

Her father would adore it, built into the tree like it was. It was almost as if one could believe a gnome lived here, or some other fairytale creature. But realistically, it was an echo of some long ago past—maybe even from before the Graven family had come. It was hard to tell how old it was. It was certainly not built with modern building techniques, instead wood and mud and tree roots.

Who were the people who had lived here? Obviously quite far from the village.

A bird squawked above her head and she looked up. The trees were tall, like a cathedral around her. The tops were so dense there was hardly any light filtering down. Why would someone choose to live here, almost like a mole in the ground?

Maybe they weren't given a choice? Maybe it was a hermit like legends of old. Maybe even moss people for all she knew. With a snort, she dismissed her silliness.

Her curiosity had cleared away the panic that had started to take root in her. She had simply gotten on a path leading to this long-forgotten cottage in the woods, a hidden place. That was why the path had been narrowing. There was no reason anyone came here.

Exactly how she'd gotten here, she didn't know, but she wasn't sorry. It was a curious sight, almost beyond her belief if she hadn't seen it for herself. If only she had brought her drawing sheets. Instead, she would have to use her memory, but it was a rich sight of something that was as otherworldly as she had ever seen.

It was cold too. The lack of sunshine protected the last vestiges of winter. Would snow even reach down here, she wondered. With her arms crossed, she returned to the sparse path and walked back the way she'd come. Before she was out of sight, she looked back on the cottage. As curious as it was, there was something uncomfortable about it, but she couldn't understand why.

Her father would certainly enjoy her drawings of it, she thought as she kept going, leaving the strange little ruin behind.

Walking, when she came to a juncture, she chose the one that looked the widest and most used, and eventually she emerged, quite suddenly, near the flower garden in the far fields. It took her utterly by surprise, but she now knew where she was and walked home, proud that she had largely kept her head straight and not run off in a sheer panic, having to be rescued from the forest.

The house was quiet. The walk had taken much longer than she'd anticipated and she was going to be late for supper if she didn't hurry, slipping through the house before Wilhelmina could find her and complain.

Just as she was sitting down, Anna arrived to dress her hair.

"Do you know if Heinrich has returned?" Aldine asked.

"Not yet," the girl said and started brushing out Aldine's hair, pulling a caught leaf from it.

"I went walking," Aldine said. Anna didn't reply, going about her duties. "I stumbled onto the ruins of a cottage in a really thick part of the forest."

"You shouldn't go there. It's bad luck to go there," Anna stated.

76

Aldine chuckled until she saw Anna's expression in the mirror, showing that she was quite serious. Well, in a way that assessment was probably right because she had a cut on her leg to prove it was a bad idea to go clambering around a ruin. Any child should be warned not to roam around a place like that.

"That's the witches' cottage," Anna said quietly.

"The witches?"

"It is said witches lived there, a long time ago. No one goes there."

"Surely no one believes such things in this day and age?" But then the people who lived here hung on to their superstitions. So was a witch a far cry from moss people?

"Oh, there are people who still believe," Anna said. "Even those who don't believe don't take chances. You don't want to be proven wrong, do you?"

"So much fear," Aldine said quietly. Even the people who didn't believe had that inherent fear of the superstitions that had been, never quite trusting their safety.

There was probably some perfectly innocent explanation, but the state of disrepair of the place did lend one to believe the fantastical. The Brothers Grimm had much to answer for, but perhaps they were simply a reflection of the fear people had of the otherworldly, rather than the other way around.

Chapter 13

WEATHER MOVED IN the next day, rain and mist, making the visibility barely beyond the edge of the lawn. The air seemed to have a heavy stickiness that clung to everything. Heinrich still left in the morning, saying he was off to the mill.

Once breakfast was done, Aldine took herself off to the corner in the salon where she drew, spending hours trying to recreate the hovel she had found in the forest. The witches' house. It echoed through her mind. Had some woman lived there, or was it assigned as the witches' house long after anyone remembered who had lived there? It was perfectly imaginable that some children would come across the ruin and assume that a witch had once lived there. What was clear was that someone who had wanted or needed to live away from others had lived there.

"Well, well," Elke said, startling Aldine with her appearance behind her. She'd been too absorbed to notice Elke walking into the room and approaching her. "The witches' house."

Turning, Aldine looked at her. "I understand that is what it's called."

"I take it you stumbled across it. Your depiction looks just like it."

"Thank you," Aldine replied to the compliment. "I came across it yesterday."

"It's not easy to find. How did you make your way there?"

"By accident. Somehow I led myself onto the path there."

"You should not get lost in these woods," Elke warned.

"Where is Wilhelmina?"

"She has taken to her room. Isn't feeling well, apparently."

"I hope it's nothing serious."

"No, of course not. Just some stomach upset, I presume." Elke sat down. "Such a dull day."

"Isn't it."

"It can go on like this for weeks. It's quite oppressive."

It felt traitorous, but Aldine was relieved that Wilhelmina was not there in the salon with them. Her presence had felt particularly oppressive lately.

"Mint tea?" Elke suggested.

"Please," Aldine said and Elke rose to go find Weber.

Putting her brush down, she left the water coloring she was doing and moved toward the seating arrangement where they normally had tea.

Elke returned a few minutes later, carrying a tea service. "I don't know where Weber is, but he's hiding somewhere. Probably takes the opportunity to hide himself away when Wilhelmina is indisposed. Luckily, I am not completely ignorant how to brew tea."

Setting it down, she poured two teas and handed one over. "Thank you," Aldine said, taking a sip of the steaming mint liquid. She was getting quite used to the taste. "The people around here are quite frightened of the ruin in the woods, aren't they?"

"They still fear the curse of the witch."

"Curse?" Aldine asked.

"Some woman they had determined was a witch way back when they feared witches, cursing the people around here. I am sure they assign Heinrich's bad luck to the curse."

"That's ridiculous," Aldine said.

"Of course it is." Placing her cup down, Elke crossed her legs under her voluminous skirt.

"What does it say exactly?"

"It isn't so much what it says. Apparently one of the distant Count Gravens did kill his wife. And now Countess Gravens have been dying again. So the belief is that the Count Graven is destined to murder his wife."

Unable to help it, goosebumps rose up Aldine's arms, because that was her. The curse people around here believed in was that Heinrich would kill her—like he had done twice before. A shudder went through her at the thought.

"And people believe this?" she asked.

"Oh yes," Elke said. "To many in the village, you are a marked woman, probably going to drop dead any minute." She said it with such a light tone, it sounded ludicrous.

"And why would he kill me?"

"Now that is less clear. Whether it is just a hidden hatred for women that comes out of him, or if the witch compels it without him quite knowing what he is doing, I don't know." Now it sounded like it was a certain he would do it. Aldine tried to shake the ill ease off her. There was no reason to feel uncomfortable because of some superstitions people had.

"And they believe he killed his other wives."

"Absolutely. Or rather the curse did."

"Who was this distant countess that had died?"

"They don't really talk about her, but it is said she was strangled by her husband on their wedding night. I don't know if that is true, but it is what is said."

"How can a man murder someone on their wedding night in a jealous rage?"

"Maybe she wasn't a virgin?" Elke offered. "Back then, losing one's chastity was tantamount to sleeping with the devil, wasn't it? The gravest of offenses."

"Is this even true?"

"Well, I would not ask Wilhelmina about it. She dislikes you enough as it is."

It was a little strange hearing it confirmed that their mother-in-law disliked her. She hadn't done anything to deserve it.

"Why Heinrich? Why the count?" Aldine asked.

"I don't know. The long history of the title, I suppose. I don't really know where the curse originated, or why it is tied to the Graven house."

"Is it, though? Or simply assigned because his wives had misfortunes."

"No the curse existed before he married. There was talk of it as he married for the first time, people saying she was signing her own death warrant by marrying him. And those people were proved right."

Frowning, Aldine didn't know what to make of this. It was strange to think that a lot of the people she saw when she left the house believed she would die soon, the victim of an old witch's curse. Her thoughts buzzed around her head as she tried to think this through, searching for the falsehoods in what she was being told—besides the fact that curses didn't exist.

"Both Heinrich and Ludwig think it's utter nonsense, of course."

"What about Wolfgang?"

A look of surprise registered on Elke's face. She dismissed him as unimportant the way Wilhelmina did. "I've never asked him. Although if anyone would wish a curse on a younger brother they believed had stolen their inheritance, then it would be the bastard older brother, wouldn't it?"

The sheer bitterness was disconcerting. Elke really didn't like Wolfgang—with a strong vehemence. That had to come from somewhere, but Aldine didn't understand where. "Why do you hate him so much?"

"Why is he still here? There is nothing for him."

"His brothers, I suppose," Aldine said. "This is still his family."

"He is illegitimate. He doesn't belong here."

"So where does he belong?"

"Who cares?" Elke spat. There was definitely something more to this than Wolfgang's birth status. Elke was reasonable with most things, except when it came to Wolfgang. "Go to the city, go somewhere. Instead, he hangs around and constantly reminds Wilhelmina about his existence. He does it on purpose, you know. Pure spite. Doesn't give a damned about Heinrich and Ludwig. Watch him. He's not here for brotherly love."

For a moment, Elke sounded a bit unhinged, but maybe there was something Elke knew about Wolfgang that Aldine didn't. It sounded that way.

"If anyone is a curse on this family, it is that man." The distress was practically dripping off Elke, this turn of conversation was upsetting her. "God knows who he is related to on his mother's side."

"What do you mean?"

Rising, Elke refused to speak about this anymore, leaving Aldine to wonder what had happened between her and her half-brother-in-law. It sounded as if something had—something bad. Granted, he wasn't much for manners, but she had never perceived anything hostile from him. Elke had obviously seen something different. On the other hand, he seemed to be the one person who wasn't hiding from her the things that had happened to the previous countesses.

One had died in a sudden fever, the other had fallen and struck her head in the forest. Both perfectly natural. Uncomfortably, she had to admit that both could be masks for something much more sinister. It couldn't be entirely ruled out that they had been murdered. Poison could cause a deadly fever and being struck on the head, well, that would be the simplest way of murdering someone, wouldn't it? Short of running them through with a sword.

Did Elke believe that Wolfgang was responsible? That would explain the vehemence against him. Although everyone else believed it was Heinrich responsible for killing his brides. A renewed shudder trickled down Aldine's spine. That simply could not be true. They were both natural, unfortunate deaths that had struck this house, and it was being twisted into something it wasn't.

If only there wasn't that little niggle in the back of her mind that refused to completely dismiss ideas such as witches and curses, black cats running across the road and even elves living in the deepest, densest parts of the forest. In her mind, she knew it was all ludicrous, but in a corner of her heart, that fear still lived that such things could be. Darkness and its agents were out to weaken them and would find any way they could to do so. Were they not being told this every Sunday, but then also told to dismiss unsavory beliefs such as elves and witches?

Chapter 14

SUPPER WAS AMUSING that night. Heinrich was in good spirits despite the solemn weather they'd had all day. He laughed and joked, and everyone at the table seemed to enjoy the evening.

There was no moon that night, so uncompromising darkness pressed on the windows, but the fire kept them warm in the salon as they sat and talked. The prices of lumber were favorable at the moment, which seemed to please everyone. It was a conversation Aldine had little to add to.

Wilhelmina looked a little pale as she had come down for supper that evening, but otherwise seemed perfectly fine. She ate very little, however, and it was clear that the evening was taxing on her. Before long, she retired and returned upstairs.

For Aldine, the mood lifted the moment the woman left, but she felt ungenerous admitting it. In truth, her own stomach had been feeling a little upset earlier. Better now with a hearty supper. A glass of claret sat in her hand and she enjoyed it. It was Italian, she had been told.

Mostly, Heinrich spoke with Ludwig about the things they had heard, seen and learnt that day. There was little from the house to report, especially after the calm and sedate day they'd had.

"Aldine has found the witches' cottage," Elke announced during a lull in the conversation and all eyes turned to her, including Heinrich's, who had only sparingly paid attention to her after seeing to her comfort.

"Such structures are dangerous," Heinrich warned. "You should show care. The wood is rotten and the stones unstable. You must never enter a ruin like that."

"I stumbled across it by accident," Aldine admitted. "I didn't go inside." Except for the first step, where she had learned her lesson. The cut wasn't hurting quite as much now, but she hadn't forgotten it. "How long ago was it since someone lived there?"

"Hundreds of years," Ludwig said.

"Who lived there?"

All were quiet for a moment, until Ludwig spoke. "It was so long ago, no one remembers. Some family, I suppose."

"Yet, people still refer to it as the witches' cottage."

"Probably more due to the remoteness of the place rather than any particular knowledge of the people who actually existed."

"There were, though, some witch trials back then," Elke added.

"I'm not a historian, so I wouldn't know what happened three hundred years ago," Ludwig added.

"There were witch trials all over the country," Heinrich said. "We had some here in the county as well."

"So someone who lived in that cottage could have been tried as a witch," Aldine said.

"It is possible," Heinrich said. "That could perhaps be the reason why people perpetuate calling it the witches' cottage. We should tear it down. It is a hazard."

"I think it's charming," Elke said. "A ruin. I understand in other parts of the continent, people pay to have fake ruins built on their lands."

Aldine had heard of the concept, although her father had never been engaged to build a false ruin. It was popular in England, she believed.

"Well, let's hope they build them sturdier than real ruins. I think I will retire as well," Heinrich said, finishing the rest of his drink and putting the glass down. That was Aldine's cue to follow suit.

*

The house was on fire again, her motions too slow to get away from the blistering heat. The distress of it was intense, but it also felt familiar, as if she'd been here before. The walls were burning, with yellow flames flaring dangerously. There was also a roaring wind through the room, but it didn't blow out the flames. They seemed separate, the wind and the fire.

All her movements were slow. Her heart raced and she wanted to run, but it was as if she was walking through water. The heat burned down her lungs, licked along her skin. Turning, she tried to find some way out of the room, but she found none. Paintings hung on every wall. Where was the door? Even the windows were shuttered. The fire wasn't going to let her escape. It didn't want her to escape.

Panic rose higher and higher. She needed to get out. The flames were coming closer and closer, and it was so hot. Turning and turning, she sought an exit, but each time she turned, she faced an unfamiliar scene. The furniture changed, the portraits changed. More of the severe, black-dressed Lutherans with their white collars and large hats. The scenes moved, but they were silent. She didn't have time to look at the curious portraits. The fire was coming closer—she had to escape.

Finally a door and she ran for it, but never seemed to get closer, frantically trying to move her legs, never quite getting the traction to move forward.

"Help," she called. "I can't get out." The fire absorbed her voice, its roar growing louder.

The door opened and she felt relief wash through her. The room was letting her out, but she could see another room beyond.

Instantly, she was there, standing in the middle of it. A larger room with people. They were all staring at her and she tried to warn them about the fire, but the words wouldn't form in her mouth. There was hatred in their eyes. They hated her. Why? What had she done?

It was cool for a moment, but hot winds flared through. It had to be from the burning room she had come from.

Then Heinrich appeared, his blond hair glistening. He looked strong and powerful, but wasn't looking at her. A torch sat in his hand. Relief. He would save her, bring her to safety. Why was he carrying a torch?

But when he looked at her, she saw the same hatred as in the people around her.

"Did you think you would get away with it?" he asked harshly.

"I haven't done anything."

A smile spread across his lips, but it wasn't a friendly one. It was malicious, that hatred still shining in his eyes. She'd never seen him like this before.

"Please, Heinrich. Help me," she called. "You're supposed to help me."

"No one can help you. No one wants to. You can't escape the curse."

Trying to move, she sought to run away, but she was being held in place. By what, she didn't know, but she couldn't move. He wasn't going to help her. He was with these people, who all wanted to see her harmed. She had to run away, but still she couldn't budge.

Reaching the torch over, he lit her skirt and it caught fire. She couldn't feel it yet, but it was coming closer and closer. All around her was fire.

"Heinrich, no!" she called, but he only stepped back and stared at the flames. They were all looking at the flames which were traveling higher and higher. The heat was building. It was starting to burn and Aldine struggled wildly. They were trying to kill her.

"No one escapes the curse," he said, almost gently now, as if trying to soothe her. No, she would not be soothed. This was the deepest betrayal.

"You can't do this," she screamed, but no one moved to help her as she tore against the binds that held her.

"Aldine!"

Frantically, she struggled as darkness descended, pressing on her. No, pressing on her arms, trying to restrain her. There was nothing but darkness and she fought. Gone was the fire and the smoke.

"You are dreaming again," the voice said. Heinrich. Soft now, without the harsh hatred.

Forcefully, Aldine pulled away from him, but he wouldn't let her.

"Awake now," he said. "Just a dream. Calm."

Her heart still boomed inside her chest, every part of her trying to fight. A dream, she told herself, trying to calm. It had been a dream and now she was awake. Even so, she wanted to run. He'd set her on fire in the dream and that panic still sat with her, even as she tried to calm herself.

"Tomorrow, we must call the doctor so he can give you something to sleep," Heinrich said. "Such nightmares. You scream and fight."

"I dreamt I was being lit on fire," she said, omitting that he had been the one who had done so.

Her breath still beating in and out of her chest, she tried to calm herself further. The bedsheets were tangled around her legs again, and she'd worked to extract herself. "I'm fine," she finally said, trying to convince herself as much as him.

"You have a furtive imagination," he said, lying down on his side of the bed again.

"I never used to." Never in her life had she had dreams like this before. The panic of it still seared her blood and fired her body, even as she tried to relax. Sweat drenched every part of her and heat still radiated from her body.

In her dream, Heinrich had been trying to kill her. Had lit her on fire and had felt she deserved it—deserved to die.

"Sleep now," he said, his voice thick with sleep again. It was clearly over for him, but Aldine lay there, still too hot for blankets, staring at the ceiling.

You can't escape the curse, the dream had said. Obviously, it was simply a reflection of the things she had learnt, but it had been so vivid, so very shocking. The heat of the flames had licked her skin, had burned and hurt. The panic had been real—panic she had never felt before, the kind where you were sure you were about to die. She'd never felt that before either.

Maybe he was right and her imagination was more compelling than she had thought possible. It didn't feel like a mere nightmare, though. It felt like a warning. That hatred in Heinrich's eyes. That scared her more than the fire. All of them had hated her, even as she didn't know the people who had been there with him. Unlike the first dream where she had seen Elke and Ludwig, this one had only been Heinrich— telling her that she wasn't going to escape the curse.

Chapter 15

AGAIN ALDINE FELT LIKE she was recovering from a fever as she sat on a bench outside the kitchen. Breakfast had been unbearable, but she hadn't wanted to stay in her room either to then suffer Wilhelmina's contempt for the next week, so she had gone downstairs and tried to eat. Now, though, with the excuse of needing fresh air, she sat on the bench that was usually a spot for staff to relax. It also assured she would not be disturbed.

The herb garden was laid out before her, although the kitchen vegetables were apparently grown somewhere else.

Closing her eyes for a moment, she stilled her mind, avoiding the things she didn't want to think about—specifically the dream that had terrorized her the night before. Her mind was tired and her body exhausted from it. Her stomach was unsettled, as if she had eaten something unpleasant, but it was probably a side effect of the distress she had felt.

The sky was gray today, the sun occasionally peeking through. It would likely rain again later. A cool breeze gently swayed her skirt and birds chirped. All around her was calm, and it soothed her. It was as far away from the scene inside her head as she could imagine.

The problem with these dreams was that they felt like no dreams she had ever had. These were not things her mind created. It felt foreign, as if they were imposed on her. As if someone else's mind was creating these nightmares for her. And Heinrich had been the villain. There was no doubt there. The hatred in his eyes. He was the one who had set her on fire, the one who all the others took their direction from. It was he that had condemned and burned her.

Scratching her head, she looked down where her toes were peeking out from under her skirt.

What did all this mean? It felt as though it had meaning, one she didn't understand—or didn't want to understand. Was this her mind concocting horrid scenarios of him being responsible for the deaths of his previous brides? Or was this something else?

If those women's deaths weren't natural, then it meant someone or something had killed them. The curse people around here believed in said it was Heinrich. Obviously, such things were ridiculous and ought to be outright dismissed. But then these horrible dreams she was trapped in. It wasn't the first time she had dreamt it either.

"Oh, there you are," the cook said, appearing at Aldine's side. A large woman with a round belly covered by a white apron. Her white cap had an edge of lace on it. "Lady Wilhelmina is looking for you."

Aldine didn't watch herself enough to suppress the groan and then blushed.

"There now. It's not so bad. No one needs to know you have been found. You just sit a while and we won't tell anyone where you are. Lady Wilhelmina can be a bit forceful. Insists on a strong hand after..." The woman drifted off and bent over one of the herb rows, picking off tarragon leaves. "Don't like hysterics, that's all."

"Hysterics?" Aldine said, unsure if she felt offended. She'd never suffered from hysterics. Wanting a moment of fresh air and peace was hardly hysterics, was it? "What do you mean?"

The woman looked over with wide eyes as if she'd been caught saying something she shouldn't. "Nothing," she said with a placating smile.

"No, please tell me," Aldine pressed. "I am struggling to understand what Wilhelmina wants from me."

"I shouldn't talk," the woman said pleadingly. "Things a new bride shouldn't know."

"Please. I know about the other brides, and I am guessing you are referring to one of them being hysterical."

Quietly, the woman picked some more leaves. "One of the previous," she said quietly so Aldine could barely hear, "at times got hysterical. Kept saying the bed was on fire."

Painful tension rose up Aldine's spine and her arms broke out in goosebumps. Her mouth had gone completely dry as she spoke again. "What did she mean?"

The cook shrugged. "Not all there, that one. Not quite right in the head. Grew more and more hysterical and Wilhelmina tried to guide her. Pretty girl, though. It was such a shame what happened to her."

"What did happen to her?"

"Fever. Come on suddenly, but she hadn't been right for a while. Shot nerves."

"And she said the bed was on fire?"

"Over and over, screamed it one day. Said no one would listen to her."

Aldine blinked, trying to understand what she was hearing. Just the word 'fire' sent alarm bells ringing through her head. Although the woman hadn't said she'd dreamt of fire; she'd said the bed was on fire. Perhaps the dreams had affected her as she'd woken, but then Aldine remembered how when she'd first arrived, she'd noted that it had felt starkly warmer closer to the bed than away from it. At the time, she had simply dismissed it as being Heinrich's body heat she had noticed, but the temperature difference had been stark.

Suppressing a gasp, Aldine put her fingers over her lips. The tension up her spine had spread up her neck and into her hair. "She'd had bad dreams," Aldine said.

"I heard whispers of it. They called the doctor to come see to her. Gave her some pills and she calmed down."

And then died, Aldine finished in her head. Blood coursed through her body and Aldine had to rise, had to move. With quick steps, she walked away from the bench and the herb garden, just needing to move.

A curse was a lot harder to ignore if other people had experienced the same thing. Was it the same thing? Had she had the same dreams? What else could a statement like 'the bed is on fire' mean?

Aldine's gut twisted in anguish. This was an indication that all this was more than some simple superstition that should be ignored. There was something here that another had experienced. The belief that these dreams were not something from her own mind solidified now. They were foreign, being imposed on her.

"There you are," Wilhelmina said from the front door. In her anguish, Aldine had walked around the house. "We'd thought we'd do some stitching. Care to join us?" It was a question, but the tone of her voice suggested it was an order. "Not a good day to go for a walk. The weather will turn at any moment."

The last thing Aldine wanted to do was go back in the house, but she couldn't stand out there like a stubborn mule. So she smiled as best she could. It wouldn't serve anyone if she gave into hysterics, even if she felt like it. "Of course," she said, making her voice sound as light and breezy as possible.

*

For a few hours in the afternoon, Aldine got to sleep in her room and she was lost the moment her head hit the pillow. Sitting through hours of embroidery had been painful for her back and fingers, and her tired mind, so sleep was more than welcome, and she slept well. No dreams, no fire—just lovely, refreshing sleep.

Refreshing might not be right, she felt a little groggy and her stomach was still a little upset, but that was perhaps not surprising as she woke with the discomfort from what she had learnt that day again came crashing down on her.

Sitting down at her dressing table, she looked at herself in the mirror. Dark circles had formed under her eyes from lack of sleep and heightened nerves. Footsteps were approaching, but they were too heavy to be Anna's. Looking over, Aldine waited to see if they passed, but her door opened and Heinrich entered.

"You're back early," she said.

Coming in, he closed the door behind them. "How are you?"

"Better after a nap," she said with a smile, turning fully to face him, but still seated.

"I have asked Doctor Hagen to come call on you."

"That is unnecessary. I am fine."

Moving closer, he sat down on the edge of the bed. "You are not. You are having nightmares at night. Hysterical dreams."

"Hardly hysterical. Simply bad dreams."

"He will give you something to calm you."

"Please Heinrich, I do not want pills and potions."

Sighing, he looked at her and all she kept thinking was if it was normal for there to be such distance between a man and a wife. Not physical distance. They were enjoying the marriage bed, but in other ways, there was distance. But what did she know about marriage—maybe all felt this way. They didn't, after all, know each other.

Aldine watched him for a moment, unsure of what she should uncover of her suspicions. "These dreams are not normal for me," she said. "I have never had nightmares before coming here."

"The forest plays with people's minds—on their fears," he said.

"They feel foreign."

"What are you trying to say?"

"I am not the only one who has had these dreams, am I?"

Rising sharply, he stood tall above her. "Don't be ridiculous. What are you trying to say?"

"Some people think there is a curse."

"There is no such thing as curses, and I am disappointed in you for believing so," he stated.

"I don't," she started, but had to check herself. She couldn't entirely defend the assertion, since learning that the woman previously sharing his bed had had the same type of dreams. "It would help me to learn what Josefina experienced."

"We are not speaking of her or anyone else. It is not right. It is the past and there is no reason to revisit it. Mr. Hagen will come and you will feel better after he attends to you. You will not be hysterical."

Truthfully, an edge of hysteria was threatening her right then, because the doctor's pills had not saved Josefina. "I am not hysterical," she repeated through gritted teeth, but Heinrich was already walking out the door.

For a moment, Aldine wished she could simply get in a carriage and ride home to Manheim, but this was her home now. Heinrich was her husband and she had no will other than what he gave her.

Chapter 16

THROUGH SUPPER, Aldine appeared as calm as she possibly could. A calmness she didn't feel on the inside, but her husband was about to drug her and that felt very frightening, because it felt as though she needed her wits about her. Something was going on in this house and it was threatening her. The last thing she needed was for her mind to be too foggy to comprehend what was going on around her.

Around the table, people spoke animatedly, laughed and enjoyed the pork they were being served. It was lovely, but Aldine's appetite hadn't fully returned, so she picked at the food, intermittently placing small pieces into her mouth.

Heinrich appeared to be his normal self and Aldine watched him as he spoke or listened. Handsome and intelligent, but what was underneath that exterior? He was the one waking her from her dreams each night; he was the one who had been there when Josefina had believed the bed had been on fire. How could he refuse to see a correlation? Had it been the same for Luise? Had she felt unnatural influences on her sleep as well? Why would he not talk about this?

"Are you alright, my dear?" Wilhelmina asked. The woman never used endearments when the men were absent from the house and Aldine knew the woman's concern was for their benefit.

"Of course," Aldine said. "The pork is wonderful. Very tasty. I will have to compliment the cook tomorrow."

"We all should," Elke said. "We should all appreciate such a skilled presentation too."

With a smile, Aldine waited until the attention was off her and Ludwig started talking about some festival in a nearby town.

After supper, they sat in the salon and the food fueled a second wind for her. A full belly and a congenial environment made her feel a little more at ease. It had been a tumultuous few days. She would be the first to admit it. It felt as though her emotion had been plucked like piano wires.

"Shall we retreat?" Heinrich asked and she nodded. He took her hand as they said goodnight to the others. "How are you?" he asked as they walked up the stairs.

"Well," she said. Had she managed to convince him that she didn't need pills to calm her?

Through the now familiar path, he led her to his bedchamber. They had never spent the night apart since the day they had married. Their nightly rituals had become familiar to her, and familiarity brought comfort, even if she didn't feel as connected to him as she'd expected. It was just that their marriage, their relationship was new—that was all. And there was so much about him she didn't know. Such as if he murdered his brides, a perverse part of her mind stated.

There was a tall dresser with a mirror in his room and she walked over and pulled out the pins holding her hair. Behind her, Heinrich pulled off his shoes and vest. Then he slowly moved over and stood behind her. "I like it when your hair is loose and wild," he said quietly, his fingers stroking along one of her tresses. "It is beautiful."

Compliments were not things he gave readily, so she appreciated it. His fingers lightly traced along her shoulder, sending goosebumps down her arms. There was something very compelling about her husband's touch. Touch had seemed like such a fraught thing as she had transitioned into a woman, but now it was abundant. She was just starting to receive it without tension. It felt like luxury. Leaning over, he kissed the base of her neck. Warm lips teased her skin, and the peaks of her breasts pebbled, rubbing against the hard confines of her stays.

But he moved away to the other side of the room, where his toiletries were and now she only saw the back of him. The broad sweep of his shoulders, the trim waist. How lucky she had been to get such a handsome husband. Looking back at herself, she wondered.

"I don't think your mother likes me," she admitted.

It took him a while to answer. "She is set in her ways and the last few years have been... tumultuous."

Aldine supposed that was one word for it. It was the most he had ever said about what had gone on before her. Quietly, she turned around where she stood and looked at him directly, but he didn't turn to her as he prepared for bed.

"You will grow to like each other. These things take time," he finally said, but there was something in his tone she didn't understand, as if he was saying something to himself that she wasn't supposed to understand. Maybe he simply didn't believe that his mother would come around. She certainly seemed to have an overbearing personality, and that wouldn't simply mellow over time, would it? "She wants what's best for me. All mothers do."

Turning, he caught her watching him, which urged her to continue with her undressing, undoing the small buttons down the side of her dress. Taking it off, she placed it neatly over the back of a chair.

Heinrich moved to help her untie the binds of her stays, releasing her lungs to breath fully. It was the loveliest part of the evening, the sign that the day was truly at an end. She could feel the warmth behind him as he stood close. Again he gently kissed her on the shoulder.

"Things will change when children come," he said. "No one has time for pettiness when there are children in a house."

Walking away, he lay down on the bed as she finished her undressing. There was a new tension in her that hadn't been there before she'd had the dream where he had purposefully been attacking her. The pure hatred in his eyes. It had been an expression she had never seen on him, so how was it that she knew what it looked like? Where had it come from?

Was the man lying in wait in the bed harboring such hatred under a mask? Or was some spirit entering him and performing dastardly deeds?

Utter nonsense, of course, but it was hard to tell that part of her brain that feared dark corners and murderous intent to stop.

Taking a deep breath, she finished her undressing and walked toward the bed and lay down. It didn't feel like it was on fire. In fact, the sheets were cold.

His hand snaked around her neck and brought her lips to his, the kiss deep and passionate. Her body formed to his, welcoming his warmth and the firm body pressed to hers. His hand urged her leg around his hip, bringing them closer. Warming heat built inside her, preparing to receive the full intimacy between a man and a woman.

With his ministrations, her nightgown pulled higher and higher, until most of her was revealed.

Could a man who hated be tender like this? She tried to look in his eyes, but they were lost with glassy desire. There was no doubt he desired her, his eyes roamed her body, until he took a hard nipple into his mouth, teasing it with his tongue, his hand kneading the other. It stoked the heat inside her, flaring the desire she was only starting to understand.

Could a man who hated her do lovemaking like this? She wasn't naïve enough to not know that men could lay with women easily and with no attachment—that lust was its own reward. That did not make him guilty of anything.

Fingers teased lower, slipped inside her. Desire flared molten inside her. How could she want him like this if there was that part of her that wasn't assured he meant her no harm? She would know—in her heart, she would know if he meant to hurt her. It was impossible to want someone who meant one harm, wasn't it?

Shifting himself, he pressed his manhood inside her, the feeling of fullness enveloping her. Sensation spread to every part of her body, making her nipples even harder and even her lips tingled. They fit so beautifully and perfectly together. The soft undulations that drove him deeper inside her, until he was fully submerged.

She could not want him like this if he wasn't true, could she? The tension built higher than it ever had before, almost painfully, but she couldn't stop—she needed more. Moans escaped her each time his hips hit home to hers. Everything about her, everything she could conceive of drew back to their joining. It filled the entirety of her. She had no defenses.

The tension culminated and for a moment, she wondered if she was in real trouble, before waves of sheer, exquisite pleasure washed over her. It ripped through her body so forcefully, it felt like she needed to face down a storm. His chest to hers, she held him as tightly as she could, fearing she would be ripped away otherwise. His powerful strokes beat into her as he reached his release, every part of his body tense with effort.

There was nothing polite or mild about this. It was base and compelling, and accessed parts of her she didn't understand. But they had done this together. They were together in this.

Breath was stolen from her body and she couldn't breathe. He pulled away from her. And finally both her blood and her breath slowed, and she truly did feel like her body was burning with heat. It was a pleasant heat, a lulling heat. The warmth of completion. Something had been completed tonight.

But she needed to know if he was there with her, but he was facing away from her, breathing deeply and frantically. He wasn't giving her his eyes, wasn't letting her look into his soul, and she needed to. She only ever had glimpses of it.

"Heinrich," she said through shaky breath.

Looking back at her, she only had his eyes for the briefest moment, before he leaned over and kissed her at the temple. It was a lovely gesture, but she felt it was in lieu of what she really needed.

Now he kissed her shoulder, his fingers entwining with hers. Again a loving gesture. Through gestures and affection, he showed her care, but she still wasn't getting something. Perhaps she was asking too much.

Chapter 17

THE CHURCH WAS ICY cold inside, the weather having turned cold outside too. A warm blanket had covered her legs on the way over, but Aldine wished she could have brought it into the church too. Instead, it sat waiting for her outside, while she froze inside, squeezing her legs tightly together to preserve her heat.

"We must not give ourselves to superstition," Reverend Stubbe declared and Aldine looked up. She'd lost track of the sermon, but this drew her attention and she listened to every word. "It is our own weaknesses that needs to be guarded against. The fight over one's soul is never outside of oneself."

It was rare that Aldine wanted more once a sermon was finished. It was normally the time she prayed for, if she were honest.

With the end, everyone rose and mingled. Reverend Stubbe first came to speak to Heinrich, being the most illustrious member of the congregation, then Wilhelmina and working his way down the line.

"Could I ask you a question?" Aldine asked when he came to speak to her.

"Of course. Come," he said, showing her toward an empty pew on the other side.

"I am sure you have heard the things said about this family—about there being a curse on the family."

The vicar watched her for a moment, as if he didn't know what to say. "As I said in my sermon, superstition is not true religion. There are no answers in such beliefs. It is all false."

With a frown, Aldine listened. "But the church has always believed in magic, in witches. If there is magic, how can there not be curses?"

With a sigh, he leaned back a little against the wooden backrest. "It is true. Martin Luther himself believed in witches, even said they had to be executed, but he also believed they could be led back into the light. He believed that there was a sphere where the devil's influence was God's will."

"God's will," Aldine repeated. Now she was more confused than ever.

"It is not in dark spells that your soul will be tested. It is within you. Luther did believe in magic, but that it has no power if one trusts in God."

That was easy to say when one wasn't the victim of it. "So curses can exist."

"Well, we don't believe such things these days. Then, as now, it is simply a belief in lost souls. People who have turned away from God. God is the only salvation."

It wasn't so much of an answer as a diversion. "So how does one combat a curse?"

In a sense, he looked a little disappointed in her, but his life wasn't on the line from some witch's curse. "Prayer," he said. "Witchcraft, any form, cannot harm a righteous man—or woman. It is nothing more than ill intent, and it cannot pierce the armor of trust in God."

On one level, she understood what he was saying, but then he cared about souls not lives. At no point had Aldine ever felt as though her soul was in jeopardy—but according to the previous Countesses Graven, her life may well be. "So a curse cannot act upon an innocent party, make them do things they don't want to?"

"No, Aldine," he said. "Magic is not real. Those who practiced it might have wanted to believe so, but it was their own souls who were in jeopardy. The things that have happened at Schwarzfeld, we must accept as God's plan."

"Then what is his plan for me?"

"That we cannot know, but we must trust."

Again, easier said than done.

"Trust and pray, Aldine, and if you still struggle, come and see me again," he said as he rose, ending this conversation. There was, perhaps, little else to say, even if she felt less assured now than a moment ago. Apparently, curses existed, but their effects were not something to worry about. Heinrich said curses didn't exist, but everyone else, even most of the people in this church believed that they did, and she was the target of it.

While the others chatted on the ride back to the house, Aldine couldn't pull her thoughts away from her predicament. She didn't know what to do—if she could simply ignore all this about a curse and burning beds and just get on with her life. But then what if her life, on its current course, was very short? What if a curse was working to kill her that very moment?

How did one simply ignore something like that? Silently, she watched the faces in the carriage with her. Heinrich and Ludwig rode horses next to the carriage, so it was only her, Elke and Wilhelmina being driven by Weber. As per usual, Wolfgang disappeared the moment the service was over and sought to spend his Sundays elsewhere. Did anyone know where he went?

Lunch was served shortly after they returned and it was a nice meal. For a moment, everything seemed calm and jovial. Even Aldine could forget everything for a moment and simply enjoy herself. Heinrich seemed happy. How could he possibly be the one who hurt these women? How could he look at her and have dark thoughts about murdering her? He couldn't. But then could a curse simply act through him, make him an unwitting conduit? Could he be doing these things and not be aware of it?

All these questions she had and no answers. Normally, she would find a book that would tell her the answers, but there weren't books for these questions. Who could she ask? The church obviously had no answers for her. Where did one find an expert on curses? This wasn't an issue she had ever dealt with in her life. Her parents would think she had lost her mind if she brought this up with them.

After sitting in the salon for a while, Aldine sought the solitude of her room. No one, other than Anna, ever came in there, and today, she sat by the fire and watched the dark, cold weather outside. Her mind was too occupied to read or draw; it wouldn't let go of this constant panic she felt inside, the urge to do something, to fight.

Her stomach clenched today, feeling out of sorts. Perhaps something from their lunch had not agreed with her. Or maybe it was simply nerves that made her feel so unsettled.

The weather outside grew darker and darker, to the point where it was hard to see dusk coming. It was simply dark one moment when she looked up.

A soft knock came at her door, and she knew it was Anna. "Come in," she called and the young maid silently entered the room.

"Do you wish me to light the lamp?" she asked. The room had grown dark too.

"Yes, I suppose," Aldine said. "I hope your walk to the house wasn't too horrid."

"It's raining a little now," Anna said, who'd just come back from her day off.

"How is your mother?" It was a guess, but where else would Anna go on a Sunday?

"She is well. Shall I dress your hair?"

Getting up, Aldine shifted to her dressing table, where Anna undid the pins holding her hair to brush it out before redressing.

"You mentioned before," Aldine started, "about people believing there is a curse on this family."

Anna remained silent, and Aldine knew she didn't like being questioned about these things.

"If I wanted to find out more about curses, who would know?"

"No one around here curses people," Anna said.

"There must be some way of breaking a curse."

Anna's eyes carefully sought her in the mirror. These things scared her and she didn't want to discuss it.

"It's just that Reverend Stubbe was little help, and I think I need help."

The maid shifted uncomfortably between her feet as she worked. "Maybe one of the elders? The Tober woman might know such things. By the look of her, she's old enough to have witnessed the witch trials. I've heard that there are some that go to her for potions."

"Potions?"

"For conceiving—or the opposite," Anna finished quietly. "She knows forest remedies."

Not exactly what Aldine wanted, but if she knew of such things, maybe she knew of curses as well. "Where is she found?"

"Some miles away in the Gelling Forest."

"She lives alone?"

"No, there is a small village there. They have lived there for a long time."

"Thank you," Aldine said, feeling like she had a lifeline. It may not solve anything, but at least she had someone to ask. Tober, this woman was called. It was the only hope she had.

Chapter 18

WITH A START, ALDINE awoke abruptly, again escaping the fire in her dreams. This time she had been running from Heinrich, feeling him chasing behind her. He'd called for her, but he hadn't meant her well.

Her heart still pounding and her lungs fought for breath, her eyes frantically searched the darkness, but the whispers in her dreams seem to have followed. It wasn't with her ears she heard them, but she still did. Whispers, too faint to understand. They were whispering about her, but she couldn't make out the words.

Her nightgown was soaked through and the blankets felt incredibly hot, so she lifted them off, but wasn't greeted by the cold air she expected. It was still hot. Flames, like she had felt in her dreams. Was she still dreaming?

"Heinrich," she said, seeing the dark form next to her, but he didn't wake.

Flames licked her skin, traveling along her body as if the bed was on fire, forcing her to jerk back.

"Heinrich," she called again and turned to shake him, but he still didn't wake. No one would sleep through that.

Whispers continued and she looked around, trying to get her ears to identify a direction, but there was none. The heat came in currents, washing over her, her skin, her lips, her eyes. The bed truly felt like it was on fire.

Scrambling out of bed, she moved away and was finally met with cold air—and silence. The room was dark and still, the floorboards cold under her bare feet. The cold air a balm to her skin and her ragged breath. Shaking fingers, she held them to her lips, her eyes darting around the room.

Stepping closer, she felt the heat again, so she backed away. It was there; it was real. Moving back, she yelped as the back of her legs struck a chair. Sitting down, she tried to get her thoughts under control. She was not asleep. This was not a dream, but the heat had followed her into waking life. There were no flames, but the bed felt as if it was on fire. Josefina had said she'd experienced the same. This wasn't just her. The bed felt like it was on fire.

Tucking her hands under her arms and crouching over, she looked back on the bed. Nothing was seen.

"Heinrich," she called, but still he didn't wake. A noise made her startle, but she realized it was coming from beyond the closed door. Disbelievingly, she stared at the door, fearing it would open, but it didn't. Getting hold of herself, she walked to the door and threw it open, seeing nothing but a dark and silent hall. There wasn't a person standing on the other side—a witch wishing them ill. There was nothing out of the ordinary.

It was even colder out in the hall and Aldine felt goosebumps rise along her arms. The fact that the nightgown was drenched didn't help.

Taking a last look, and hoping deep in her heart that she didn't see anything that shouldn't be there, she returned to the bedroom and closed the door. Placing her head on the door, she closed her eyes, not knowing what to do. Something was going on—something dark and harmful. It was either centered around the bed or around Heinrich. Whatever it was affected him, because he would not rouse.

Turning back, she stared at the bed. It looked so innocent, just a bed in the darkness with the sleeping form of a man. Slowly, taking a step closer, she tried to feel for the heat, but it wasn't there. Whatever it was, it had passed. No more heat, no more whispers.

Her arms wrapped around her, her eyes searched the room for something out of place, but saw nothing.

"Heinrich?" she called and finally he moved.

"What?" Whatever had held him asleep had lifted too. "What are you doing out of bed?"

"It was here, the curse."

With a groan, he turned on his stomach. "Just go back asleep. You were dreaming."

"I was not."

But she did as she was told and crawled back under the sheets. The damp nightgown made it uncomfortable, but she waited a while until he was asleep before taking it off and letting it drop to the floor. Every night, she seemed to have to strip off her nightgown.

What she really wanted was to be held, but she'd heard the annoyance in Heinrich's voice, so she tucked the blankets closer to her and tried to feel comfortable in a bed that had the habit of trying to burn her.

Too much had happened for all this to be dismissed. She hadn't imagined the heat, or the whispers. A shudder passed through her at the thought. What were those whispers? Who were the people whispering? Were there ghostly presences watching them as they slept?

Discomfort turned her stomach and she had to close her eyes, but also feared what went on around her if her eyes were closed. But there were no more whispers, or heat. In fact, the bed didn't seem to get warm at all. Her feet felt frozen, almost painful as she struggled to get heat into them.

For a moment, misery got the better of her and all she wanted to do was run away and go home, but this was her home now. With this husband who didn't believe her that something strange and otherworldly was happening. If just morning would come. Light would chase all this darkness away, but there wasn't even a hint of light through the window.

Aldine was awake when Heinrich woke, the sun having slowly crept in through the window. Sleep had been hard to get and she had lain there staring at the ceiling for what seemed like hours.

Heinrich rose and started dressing. "I will call for the doctor today."

"This isn't me," Aldine said, sitting up in bed.

"These dreams are stopping you from sleeping."

"It wasn't dreams," she said. "Yes, dreams, but it was here when I woke. I could feel the fire. I heard whispers. I tried to wake you—you wouldn't wake. I shook you."

"You're being hysterical. It was a dream and you are giving yourself over to nonsensical fantasy."

"I am experiencing the same thing Josefina experienced. Exactly the same. Isn't that curious to you?"

"No!" he said harshly. "I don't know what it is you want from me? I give you as much attention as I can."

"Attention?" she said incredulously. "This isn't about attention. I don't want to die like all other of your brides. Something is happening here."

"Nothing is happening here, other than you being overwrought and neurotic." Grabbing his jacket, he stormed out of the room.

"Which in this house seems to come before death," she said to the door that just slammed shut. He didn't believe her, that much was clear. What more proof did he need? From his perspective there was no proof—except two dead brides. Would he take it seriously when he was burying her? All the good it would do her then.

Exhaustion made her sluggish and miserable as she lay back down on the bed. Tears flowed down into her hairline. Her stomach was still an uncomfortable twist of nerves and ill ease. And soon she would have to face a doctor to treat her neurosis. God knew what he would do.

How had this marriage turned into an utter nightmare? But she had a lifeline, this woman, Tober. Firstly, though, she didn't know where this woman lived, and she had no means of getting there. She could just imagine the look she would get if she asked Wilhelmina, or even Elke.

Sleep was not going to come, she determined, so she got up and went through the door leading to her own room, where Anna had already lit a fire for her. Lying down on the bed, the exhaustion weighed down every part of her body. Could she insist she sleep in her own bed tonight? Whatever this was seemed tied to Heinrich, or his bed. Was she safer sleeping in another bed? Would the dreams leave her, the heat and the whispers? If it was the first time this had happened, she would question her own senses, but she had felt it when she'd first gotten here, and now that she knew others had felt it too, it only confirmed something was very seriously amiss—except no one believed her.

Anna's soft knock sounded at the door, coming to help her dress. It would be another day of sheer exhaustion, and it was a good six hours until she could retreat back here for a nap. Napping in her own bed during the day had never given her any trouble, but the nights—they were horrendous, and they seemed to be getting worse.

How could she beseech Heinrich to understand? How could she prove that this wasn't in her head? But he didn't even want to listen to her, dismissed her the moment she uttered something about it. And now they'd had harsh words. He'd called her overwrought and neurotic. Anyone who knew her would never accuse her of that—didn't he understand that? She wasn't a woman to give herself over to fanciful ideas. But every night, she dreamed of fire and awoke drenched in sweat.

Could she be wrong? Could this be her and her nerves were getting the better of her? It would be the logical conclusion over some age-old curse enacting its evil from the distant past. Still, she was going to find this Tober woman.

Chapter 19

TRUE TO HIS WORD, the doctor came. Hagen his name was, a neatly dressed young man with wavy hair. Heinrich wasn't there, but they met him in the salon. Wilhelmina had taken it upon herself to direct him, telling him that Aldine was having nightmares that stopped her from sleeping properly. Overwrought nerves were mentioned a few times. Apparently, her participation in this wasn't necessary. They spoke about her as if she wasn't there.

Elke smiled intermittently, sitting quietly and listening to Wilhelmina and the doctor speak. At times their voices were hushed as if they didn't want her to hear what they were saying. Heinrich's concern was mentioned.

With her head held high, there was nothing Aldine could do but sit there and let them talk about her. It was Heinrich's responsibility to see to her if her health was in jeopardy, even if he refused to listen to her concerns.

Had this happened to Josefina too? There was mention of her being given pills and potions for her nightmares. The fact that she had died from a fever sent a thrill of fear down Aldine's back, the thought of lying in bed and burning up. She had some measure of what that felt like, the pervasive and piercing feeling of being trapped, of the heat refusing to relent.

As she watched, Doctor Hagen leaned over his black doctor's bag and pulled out a bottle of pills, which he handed to Wilhelmina. "This should calm her nerves," he said. Biting her tongue, Aldine stopped herself from expressing that she was perfectly calm. They weren't interested. This was

Heinrich's command and it was him they took direction from.

Coming over, the doctor sat down on the small footstool next to her. He smiled calmly. "These will make you feel better. They calm nerves and will induce sleep."

Keeping her tongue, she smiled back, fearing that if she relayed what she truly believed, he would recommend that she be hauled off to a madhouse. The last thing she wanted was to be deemed the troubled wife who needed more direct medical supervision. No sane person would seek that fate—to be experimented on with potions and terrifying lunacy treatments. Perhaps she was overreacting a little, but everyone heard the stories of 'touched' wives who spent the rest of their lives in madhouses.

"Take two," he said, holding out two pills in his hand and a glass of water in the other, waiting patiently for her to take them. Both Wilhelmina and Elke stared at her until she took them and put them in her mouth. "And let's see that they went down well enough," he said and Aldine's mouth drew tight until she relented and opened her mouth like a child so he can see that she'd really swallowed them. Already she was being treated like a mad woman, all control being taken away from her.

The pills had not started acting by the time he left, but soon after, a dullness descended on her, making her thoughts and her movement lethargic. It felt as though she barely had control over her fingers and almost as if she was trapped in her body. She could neither read nor paint, could only sit there and stare at the walls. It was awful.

Elke was embroidering beside her and eventually made some mint tea for them. Even the flavor tasted strange in Aldine's mouth. Whatever this drug was, it was awful. Thoughts refused to form and for hours, she sat there, utterly unable to do anything.

Shortly before supper, the effect started to give. "I might stretch my legs," she said and rose from her chair.

"As you please," Wilhelmina said and Aldine walked outside into the fresh air. She felt like crying; she felt like running away, but not only was she stuck in this house, she was now imprisoned in her own body. Her mind wasn't recovered, still muddled and she wandered to the stable with some notion of saddling a horse and riding back to Manheim.

But Wolfgang was there and she hadn't expected him to be. Foiled. Looking over, he considered her for a moment. "What's wrong with you? You look like you've seen a ghost."

"The doctor came and gave me calming pills," she admitted sluggishly.

Lifting his saddle off, he carried it to the tack room. He came back and gave the horse a portion of hay.

"Apparently this house will be less—" she started before stopping herself. *Haunted* was what she was going to say.

"Less what?"

"Isolated," she said instead. He eyed her suspiciously. He didn't like her, but he was the only person who truthfully answered her questions. Although he seemed to have no qualms over that truth hurting. "There is a woman, Tober, she is called. Who lives in Gelling Forest. Do you know her?"

"What would you want with someone like that?" he said, even more suspiciously.

"Did Doctor Hagen come and give any of Heinrich's other wives pills?"

"Not that I know of. Along with their heartfelt feelings, they didn't exactly share their health concerns with me."

Is Heinrich trying to kill me, was what she really wanted to ask, but he would think her a complete lunatic, who probably needed calming pills that turned her into something close to an imbecile.

Her thoughts were wandering. "Conception potions," she said. "I've learned this woman does them."

For a moment, he considered her. God knew what went through his mind, but for some reason, she didn't want to admit the real reason she wanted to see this woman. Someone in her position, a new bride, would be concerned with conceiving. The joy of this marriage to the family would soon falter if she didn't conceive. Her esteem with Wilhelmina would plummet even further.

"Gelling Forest is not close enough to walk to."

"Then I must take a carriage."

"Do you even know how to steer a carriage?"

"Enough to manage."

With a sigh, he turned to her. "I am going that way tomorrow. I can take you. I'm assuming Heinrich has given you his blessing for doing this?"

Awkwardly, she nodded. Somehow, she had to get Heinrich to agree to her going to this woman's house, or in that general direction. He would be eager for her conceiving as well, but she could well imagine that he wouldn't put much stock in a woman who peddles in forest herbs.

*

The doctor was right in that she slept through the night. Slept might not have been the right word. There had been no dreams at all—she had simply ceased to exist for eight hours. The devil himself could have pranced around the room and she would not have noticed, which made her concerned about what had happened while she had been absent from her mind and body. Was this how one died of a fever, she wondered as she woke, feeling so sluggish and groggy, she could barely stand.

As Heinrich was about to leave, she muttered something about going to Gelling on church services, and that Wolfgang had offered her a ride. He paused for the moment before mumbling something about it being good she did community work, but she heard the word 'fine', and that was all she needed.

Her scalp felt completely detached from her head as Anna came to do her hair, feeling none of the tugs and pins. Anna had to physically help her dress, which was both embarrassing and distressing.

After a quick breakfast where she couldn't bring herself to eat, she excused herself, saying she was going for a ride to see more of the countryside and wished to stop by the church to see Reverend Stubbe. Grudgingly, Wilhelmina accepted this, but was less than enthusiastic about Wolfgang's offer to take her on his errand.

Technically, he was her brother-in-law, and could be trusted with her care and chaperoning. Wilhelmina's distrust of him obviously didn't extend to worrying about him ravaging his sister-in-law, or else the woman didn't care. Or was that her lethargic mind being ungenerous?

Wolfgang wasn't enthusiastic about seeing her when she appeared in the stable, but he didn't go back on his word. "I didn't take you for one who put stock in snake oils and witch potions."

"There were a lot of things I didn't put stock in before coming here," she muttered more to herself than to him, but here she was lying to everyone to go see some old woman about breaking a curse on her husband.

They drove for a while, far off Heinrich's land. They spoke little on the way, and apparently they had reached their destination because he stopped in the middle of nowhere. "Down that path," he said, pointing to the side of the road.

"I will need to travel back in half an hour. Don't make me wait."

Or what, she wanted to challenge. Was he going to leave without her? If not Wilhelmina, Heinrich would likely have his hide. It was an empty threat, but what point was there in telling him. She needed Wolfgang on side to tell her the truth. It was a rare commodity and she needed to preserve her source, so she smiled. "I will do my best to be back right here within that time."

Chapter 20

THE PATH LED TO A valley where half a dozen houses were scattered around. Closest was a small cottage where the door was open and Aldine approached. "Mrs. Tober?" she called into the darkness inside.

It was quiet for a while before a clanging noise as if something fell to the ground. "Who's there?"

"Aldine Graven," she said. "You don't know me——"

"The new countess?" the woman said, suddenly appearing in the doorway. Gray hair was tied back into a thin ponytail and her face was wrinkled with age and toil, and she wiped her hands on her apron that had last been clean some time ago.

The countess title was still something she was getting used to. She wasn't one of those persons who reveled in a title. It felt too grand for her. "Yes," she replied and the woman looked her up and down without hiding it.

"What can I do for you?"

Aldine looked around and saw there was no one watching them. "Can I come in?"

For a moment, the woman seemed to weigh her request. "Does your husband know you are here?"

"Not exactly. Well, not exactly for what purpose."

With a raised eyebrow, the woman stepped back and gave her entrance. There were herbs drying on racks above her head. Everything inside the cottage was made of wood, some areas smudged with age and dirt. Even with her more simpler upbringing, it was hard for Aldine to imagine someone living here, but this woman did.

A cat jumped up and sat down on his haunches, appraising the new visitor.

"Whatever it is you're taking, you should stop," the woman said while Aldine was considering the surroundings.

"Apparently my nerves have gotten the better of me."

"Is that so?" the woman said derisively. "Men and their pills."

"I don't have much time. I wondered if you could tell me about breaking a curse."

The Tober woman smiled. "You are a believer in such things?"

"Recently, I have seen things that have made me question a great number of things." Turning her attention back on the woman, Aldine waited, wishing her mind wasn't so dampened.

"Depends on the nature of the curse."

"Frankly, I don't know the nature of the curse. I don't know anything about it other than everyone Count Graven marries seems to die suddenly and unexpected."

Walking over to a chair, the woman sat down with what looked like painful knees. "It takes a lot of energy to sustain a curse," she finally said.

"Do you believe such things exist?"

"I do," she said, but she didn't say much else.

Now, Aldine didn't know how to proceed. "Well, how do I break it?"

"Easiest way is to ask forgiveness for whatever trespass you have done."

"I haven't trespassed upon anyone. I'm not even from here. I am fairly sure Heinrich hasn't trespassed either." Although how could she know that for sure? Who knew what he'd done in his life to trespass upon someone? It was hard to see. He was mostly kind and considerate to everyone—except when it came to her claims.

"I believe the curse is inherited and was originally set upon Johannes Graven," the woman said.

The portrait of the solemn man from Heinrich's study entered her mind. This was news. Nothing of this had been said before. "Johannes Graven," she said. "So nothing to do with Heinrich."

"Curses can persist."

"How do I break it?"

"It is not you that needs to ask for forgiveness."

"But it is not Heinrich either."

"No, but he is a proxy, a descendant of Johannes."

"Witches," Aldine said. "There is a derelict cottage on the property that people refer to as the witches' cottage."

The woman shifted in her chair. "They were burned," she said and Aldine's eyes widened. Her sluggish mind tried to race through the implication. Fire. They had been burned. Of course, she knew that there had been witches burned all over the country in the olden days. Her dreams were full of fire. It was the fire that had come for them, had killed them. And she felt that fire coming closer, licking her skin. It was what they had experienced.

Her mind reeled and she her knees felt a little unstable for a moment.

"Johannes Graven was the witch hunter," the woman continued. "It is common knowledge that they cursed him."

"I wasn't told," Aldine said.

"They have distanced themselves from such things, as most people have, but the past forms the present."

Aldine needed to sit down. "They cursed the family and now Heinrich is being targeted by it. He doesn't believe in it."

"Oh, he would know the stories from that time."

"Those poor women," Aldine said, unable to imagine being dragged out and burned by one's neighbor. They were probably just women going about their business, but then they had enacted a curse that was still in place some three hundred years later. Maybe they really were witches. Still, being burned at the stake was horrendous. Aldine's stomach revolted, turning as she tried to imagine what that had to feel like. The sense of betrayal from her dreams made sense now. Heinrich had been there, carrying a torch with sheer hatred in his eyes. Had that been what they had experienced?

"I don't want to die," Aldine said after a while. "This was in the past, and no one here is responsible for the suffering that was endured then."

"Power is stored somewhere," the woman said. "In a talisman. Often buried, sometimes not. Something that persists."

With intent, Aldine listened to every word. "A talisman. What would it be?" This was so very far from the things that were familiar in her life, she felt like a stranger in a foreign world.

"It could be anything. It would have been something that represents the women. And it would be nearby."

"Nearby," Aldine repeated. There were so many old things in the house it was hard to even think of them all. Something imbued with their power, with this curse. "So if I find it and destroy it, the curse will dissipate?"

"Yes," the woman said.

"And it was something of theirs?"

"Not necessarily, but it would represent them."

Well, that was helpful, she thought sarcastically. What in the world could represent witches in that house? "You also said buried."

"It is tradition that a talisman can be buried near where they wish to act."

"How would I ever find it?"

"Is there anywhere that the curse seems to be particularly focused?"

"The marriage bed," Aldine admitted. "All seem to be focused there."

"Then it is nearby you should look. A dousing rod can be used."

"Dousing rod," Aldine repeated, recalling what she had always throught was quackery. "How does one use a dousing rod?"

"Hold it and let it lead you where it will."

Blinking, Aldine stared at the woman. It still felt like this was all about a different language that she didn't understand and didn't want to, but her life was on the line. She had to break this curse, because it was trying to kill her.

"And stop taking whatever it is you're taking. There is a scent about you—a bad one. It is not serving you well and you will grow sick if you continue."

That was easier said than done. They were watching her like a hawk, making her take the pills. Somehow she needed to deceive them. "Thank you," she finally said. "This has been helpful."

"Good luck," the woman said as Aldine rose and moved to the door. Nodding, she moved through the door into the sunshine. Again, it felt as if the story of everything she knew had changed. The Gravens were the witch hunters who had burned women at the stake. That was their history, and that history was still haunting them to this day—even if they refused to admit it.

Walking back up the valley was harder than coming down, but she did it and waited by the road for Wolfgang to return. Apparently, speaking to Mrs. Tober had only taken a few minutes, so now she had to wait for what seemed like a long time.

Her mind was still trying to absorb what she'd learnt. It explained so much about the dreams, about what was happening, and now she had to find a talisman that was powering this curse. Something that was close to where the trouble was, which was the marriage bed.

Wolfgang appeared, looking stern as he always did. Like Heinrich, he came from a line of witch hunters, men who had condemned women to a torturous fate. "Got what you came for?"

"No, she said it was too early in the marriage to resort to such things. To let nature take its course first." It amazed her how easily she'd just lied. It had slipped out smoothly and he seemed to believe her. With a smack on the horse's rump, they set off home. As she drove away, she looked back down the valley where the houses couldn't be seen from the road. That woman, Tober, was exactly the kind that would be accused by witch hunters in the days when such accusations were laid. She would burn at the stake for what she did with potions and herbs. It was a curious and uncomfortable thought.

Chapter 21

THE WEATHER CLEARED up the next day, producing sunshine again, but the house seemed darker than ever—at least to Aldine. A big chapter in the Graven family's long history was now written into the very wood and fabric of this house. And very little of it had been mentioned within the family. It was as if it wasn't even thought about.

The paintings on the walls took on new meaning. They were scenes from that period. Village scenes. Aldine studied them with renewed interest and concern, but they didn't reveal anything shocking or sinister—simply scenes. People standing around and talking, the village communing. Although now she knew what they were communing about.

After breakfast, she went into Heinrich's empty study and viewed the portrait of Johannes Graven. Long, curly hair reached his shoulders, light brown by the look of it. His eyes seemed harsher than the other time she'd seen this portrait. This was a man who had condemned and then murdered women—his neighbors effectively. Had he grown up next to that family and then turned on them? They had been defenseless against him.

Then again, they could have been true witches as their curse seemed to persist to this day. A shudder went through her body. Murder was so brutal, so unforgivable and unnecessary, but these women were responsible for a few deaths of their own. And they now threatened her.

Looking around the room, she viewed the artifacts, but couldn't see anything that looked suspicious. It would help to know what she was looking for, but she didn't. Something that represented them—the witches. From the sounds of it, there was more than one, although she didn't know how many that man had condemned to burn at the stake.

From her dreams, she had some semblance of how horrible such a fate would be. She felt their anguish and grave disappointment. It was hard to comprehend that someone could be so callous as to stand by and watch someone burn to death, but apparently that man was. It was hard for Aldine to look at him. The hate in Heinrich's face from her dreams had been his hate. He'd hated these women, and Aldine had trouble understanding it.

She'd already been through the bedroom, which had remarkably little in it other than toiletries and the washing stand. Heinrich wasn't someone who liked his bedchamber cluttered. There was nothing really that represented them. There wasn't even really anything old in the room except for the bed itself, the frame being finely carved in dark wood that was almost black with the oils and varnish kneaded into it over who knew how long. Was that bed from the time Johannes had lived? Could it be imbued with the witches' curse?

The carvings were mainly of leaves and acorns. There was nothing sinister in the carvings. She'd looked over the whole bed. But then would it have to be a depiction of something sinister? She hadn't thought to ask Mrs. Tober.

Leaving the study, Aldine shut the door. She didn't like the room now, didn't like how that man surveyed the space as if it was his domain. This had been his domain at one time. This family were directly connected to that man. They had to know what he'd done back then.

"There you are," Elke said, appearing out of the salon doorway. "What are you doing?"

"Nothing in particular," Aldine said. "Just wandering, I suppose."

"Come into the salon. Wilhelmina is preparing some of the flowers."

Aldine noted that it was a task Wilhelmina had never sent her way again, after she proved to be quite good at it— not that she had received any compliments for it.

"One of my magazines arrived with the mail. You can have a look through it if you like," Elke offered. Elke liked the fashion depicted in there and studied and emulated them when her magazines arrived. They described everything from dress cuts, accessories and even household management for the modern woman. The dresses were typically too fine for everyday use. "I am thinking about having a new dress sewn. There is a woman not far away who sews sufficiently well. There is a ball later in the autumn, which we all go to. Do you have a dress?"

"Yes," Aldine said. There were a few ballgowns in her wardrobe.

"I see," Elke said, almost a little tartly.

"My father's guild held them a few times each year. And there were often balls associated with the completion and opening of buildings."

"Seems you quite familiar with balls. I doubt our simple country ball will rival what you are used to."

At times, it felt as if she couldn't win. It also seemed that the reality of her more humble origins wasn't reflected in her lifestyle to the degree that both Elke and Wilhelmina expected. Being of a lower social order, she was supposed to be less skilled and having led a less elegant life, but that simply wasn't the case. Merit and birthright were at times at odds with the expectations of some. It would perhaps be best if Aldine didn't mention that she and her parents had once been invited to a royal ball—in reality a crowded, hot and not particularly amusing affair.

Ludwig joined them for lunch that day, which was a welcome addition by all. Apparently, his work with the accounts was all up to date, so he returned to spend the afternoon with his lovely ladies, he said. It was a quick lunch and Elke and Ludwig withdrew to their room to rest in the afternoon, leaving Aldine to sit with Wilhelmina.

"Have you taken your medicine?" Wilhelmina asked, putting aside her perusal of Elke's magazine.

"Yes, of course," Aldine lied. As much as she could get away with not taking it, she would, because it left her feeling utterly awful. Luckily, no one in the house insisted on checking that she swallowed like the doctor had done, so she could safely store the pills under her tongue until she could rid herself of them out the window. She had to take care, though, or someone would eventually notice the collection of white pills under her bedroom window.

In fact, she should go out there and trample them into the dirt. It was a sunny day. As she looked, she saw Wolfgang riding around the edge of the yard toward the stable. She hadn't seen him since that ride to Gelling Forest. Quickly, he disappeared from view. She chose to stay put for a while so Wolfgang was clear of the stable. For some reason, she didn't want to encounter him at the moment, although she wasn't entirely sure why. Perhaps because she had given him ammunition to use against her, because he knew where she had been that day and no one else did. If he was inclined to, he could figure that out and she didn't want to give herself the opportunity to be disappointed with him. The other women's wariness and even disgust with him was still a concern, because she didn't really know where it stemmed from, other than his simple presence.

Given sufficient time, she rose. "I might walk a little," she said, hoping Wilhelmina would not offer to join her. It hadn't happened before, but there could always be a first time, and Aldine wanted to be alone.

It was warm enough that she didn't take her jacket. She wasn't intending on going far. Strolling out of the door, she welcomed the sun, even as she was dressed warmly that day.

A knock at the window behind her had her turning back, at the same time, a whoosh and a thud sounded. It had been close, very close, whatever it was. Turning, Aldine looked back and saw a stone embedded into the lawn.

If she had not turned back, that stone would have hit her on the head. Looking up, she searched for where it had come from, but there was nothing along the roofline. Yet it had fallen. Nothing looked undisturbed.

She'd almost just died and her mind was screaming at her. Absently, she jerkily stepped backward across the lawn.

Looking back, she saw Wilhelmina at the window, her eyes large and her mouth open. She had seen it. Aldine simply stared at her, not knowing what else to do.

Again she looked back at the roofline, but nothing moved up there. No shadows, no face looking down. Could it simply have fallen? Fallen exactly where she had been a millisecond prior.

Even now she felt a memory of the draft from the stone coming past her head, heard the noise of it hitting the lawn.

Wilhelmina appeared out of the door, looking up at the roof, searching for the culprit or the risk. "Come," she said, taking Aldine's wrist and pulling her away from the house. "The house is old. I'll have the men check the roofline. Weber!" she called loudly. She wasn't letting go of Aldine's wrist and Aldine was too stunned to do anything but stand there. "Weber!" she called even louder, until the old retainer appeared. "A stone fell off the roof."

As with everyone before him, he looked up and searched. "I can't see anything."

"You will have to go up there and check the house is secure. It is an old house," she repeated.

That could not have been an accident, Aldine thought. It had been so close. If not for her attention being drawn away, she would be dead now. Looking over at Wilhelmina, she realized that the woman had saved her life—completely unwittingly, but responsible all the same.

There was still a grave look on her face. She'd never seen Wilhelmina this agitated before. It was just the two of them on the lawn, both too afraid to step closer to the house.

"It almost killed me," Aldine said, her voice shaky with nerves. "If you hadn't knocked on the window, it would have hit me." She could almost see herself lying dead on the lawn, her head bloody.

"I just thought you needed your jacket," Wilhelmina replied quietly, her countenance still showing her shock.

"I was so close to not needing anything ever again."

They looked at each other. "I am sure the winds dislodged it."

It was a fairly substantial stone for the wind to dislodge. Surely something that size balancing precariously on the edge of the roof would have been noticed. No, this wasn't an accident; it couldn't have been.

The house looked large in front of her, and Aldine almost expected to see something sinister gazing at her from one of the windows, but as she searched, she saw nothing out of the ordinary.

Chapter 22

EVERYONE WAS GATHERED in the salon, including Heinrich and Wolfgang. They all spoke and commented on what had happened. Aldine was still shocked, while Wilhelmina kept pushing the calming pills on her. The last thing she wanted now was to feel utterly addled. A stone had just about dropped on her head and killed her. Something or someone in this house had done it.

Wilhelmina hadn't. That was what Aldine knew for sure. Could it have been the curse moving a stone so it fell? Or did it act through someone? That person had to be in this room. Her dreams told her it was Heinrich, but he'd been away from the house—or at least that was how it appeared. Elke and Ludwig had been in their room, which left Weber and Wolfgang.

It was hard to imagine Weber doing something like that, but then he'd been in the house. He, as opposed to Wolfgang, was not aligned with the family and the person who had acted against the witches. While illegitimate, Wolfgang was.

Watching him, she tried to see some evidence that he had come into the house and made his way to the roof. Or perhaps he didn't need to enter the house. Could he scale the outer wall to the roof?

There was no evidence in his eyes or movement, but then it could be that the person responsible didn't even know what they were doing. And now they had tried to kill her. It was almost inconceivable if it wasn't for the fact that she had felt how close that stone had been to striking her.

In a way, it made sense that it was Wolfgang, because he was the oldest. Because, would witches casting curses be specific enough to specify that it be a legitimate son that it acted on?

"Are you alright?" Elke asked sitting down next to her. "Such an unthinkable accident. It was lucky it didn't strike you."

Aldine could only nod.

"Heinrich and Ludwig are talking about going up on the roof and checking everything is secure. It must have been the storm not so long ago that had shifted the stone. And the wind recently, topping its balance. The merest wind and it toppled."

Somehow, Aldine couldn't bring herself to believe that the wind had shifted that stone, but then, she was thinking that a centuries-old curse had.

Rising, Elke walked over to Ludwig and Heinrich took her place. Taking her hand, he held it for a moment. "We will check to ensure nothing like that will happen again. I am sorry you received such a fright. That part of the house is quite old."

Was that what he explained it as? Simply bits falling off an old house? Even as he held her hand, she felt remote and distant from him. A stone nearly falling on her was not enough to convince him that something was acting against her. At risk with his belief was her life.

Wolfgang stood with his arms crossed, listening as Heinrich spoke, before they all walked out of the room, presumably to carry out this survey of the roof.

"Perhaps we should call Dr. Hagen," Wilhelmina proposed.

"No, I'm fine," Aldine replied before the suggestion took root. "I just want to rest for a while." What she really wanted was to be alone, and she rose before anyone thought to argue with her and walked up the stairs to her bedchamber. It really was the only place she felt able to breathe at the moment. Walking outside had done that for her before, but now she had to fear falling missiles aimed at her.

Pacing her room, she wondered if she should write her father, but what could he tell her. It was not his place to give her direction anymore. The truth, however, was that she didn't trust the direction given to her. She didn't trust a single person in this house. This house was run on denial, and she was guided by that denial.

Taking a deep breath, she tried to refocus. It could be that all here were innocent and this was the curse acting upon this house—a curse lodged in a talisman. The hunt for it should be her priority, and from what the Tober woman had said, it was close to where it enacted, which was Heinrich's bed.

There was an attic above it, and a storage room below it. Clearly nothing in the storage room would serve as a talisman, but what was in that attic? Could there be anything stored up there, mere feet from the bed, radiating out its evil?

Outside of the room, she heard the men come down the stairs from that very attic. As she listened at the door, she heard them keep going and it was soon silent. She had a good idea where the attic was now. It wasn't something she'd ever thought about before. Taking a deep breath, she steadied herself. It could be that she was just about to face down witches. Would there be a fight for the talisman? Did they have protection? The last thing she needed was seeing an old ghost materializing. She wasn't sure she could cope with such an occurrence. This was all terrifying enough without seeing the enemy, but what else could she do? This talisman needed to be destroyed.

Cracking the door to her room open, she saw no one outside and silently walked to the staircase leading up to the servant's floor, then up to the attic. The narrow stairway was hidden from plain sight, but she knew where it was now. The wood creaked slightly as she walked and if anyone was in the room next door, they would hear. The door was non-descript with a porcelain knob.

The knob was cold to the touch as Aldine reached for it, the ratchets of the lock clicking as it turned, then stopped. Surely they hadn't locked it? A bit more pressure and it gave, the door creaking loudly as it swung open. A rush of stale air swept by her. Distinct columns of light flowed from the windows in an otherwise dark space. Everything was bare wood with no embellishments.

There was the eerie stillness of a place not used to having people. Those places had a wildness to them, just like the witches' cottage, where that wildness was tearing the place down. The corners of the attic were shadowed and Aldine refused to let her attention linger there, in case something moved. It felt as if her attention would goad that into happening, as if her fear would bring her worry to life.

No, she was being silly. It was simply an attic. Nothing more. With all her heart, she hoped so as she stepped into the space, trying to calm her nerves.

Sheets were draped over objects and a layer of dust covered everything. There were footsteps through the dust toward a small door across the space. That was obviously the roof access, through which so many people had gone, including whoever had aimed that stone at her. It was too trampled to tell who could be responsible.

Right now, though, she was here for the talisman that caused all the trouble and she walked in the other direction, toward above where Heinrich's room was. It was hard to make out exactly, but she estimated and found a small round table with some objects. A vase and an old lantern. There was also a trunk that didn't look as old as some of the other things. Why would that be here?

Bending down, she saw that it had no lock. What could is possibly contain? Was there something in there that represented the witches? Because there wasn't much else around here, nothing that seemed from that era. Just a chinoiserie vase and a brass lantern with a cracked glass panel, so it had to be in this trunk. It wasn't even wood, instead some manufactured material. This trunk couldn't be more than a few decades old at the most, which didn't mean that its contents were similarly recent.

Pushing on the lid, it refused to give. With her fingers under the lid, she pulled, but it still wouldn't give. The lid was too tight to really get a good grip on it. But she had to see what was in that trunk. Looking around, she searched for something, her eyes traveling the space. A wardrobe stood along the wall in the distance, and a copper fire extinguisher. Also, some kind of chaise lounge covered in a sheet.

A figure made her heart stop painfully in her chest until she realized it was her own reflection in a half-covered mirror. Her groan of relief echoed back at her. With heart still racing powerfully, she tried to calm herself, wiping her clammy hands on her skirt. Every nerve in her body stood on edge.

She had to focus.

The space wasn't packed with things, but unwanted things were placed up here. Mostly things that looked intact, but perhaps not in fashion. Aldine could well imagine something unfashionable deeply offending Wilhelmina.

There was nothing to help with the lid, so she tried again, concerned she might rip a nail, but she needed to get that trunk open. Putting all her strength into it, it gave suddenly, which made her fall back jarringly on her backside onto the dusty floor.

Scrambling up on her knees, she rose and looked down into the trunk, which revealed endless bound bundles of paper and ledgers. On closer inspection, it was the household accounts, neatly stacked by years. Nothing close to the diabolical contents her mind had imagined. This was Ludwig's storage for his completed yearly accounts. Hardly the domain of witches and curses.

There was nothing in there that could represent a talisman. Like with the trunk itself, nothing inside was of any remarkable age.

Rising, she snapped the lid shut with her foot, unsure if she was relieved or disappointed. There was nothing here. Picking up the vase, she looked at the bottom and saw it had been produced by a porcelain house in Austria. Again, not particularly old, but clearly not up to Wilhelmina's taste.

"What are you doing?"

Her startle made her drop the vase, which smashed to the ground. Turning, she saw Wolfgang standing by the door to the roof. He'd been up there, while she'd assumed he'd come down with the others. A mistaken assumption on her part.

He watched her intently, then the pieces of the vase on the floor.

"Heavens you scared me," she said. That did not address his question and she struggled to state a reason that wasn't talisman hunting. "Just curious, I suppose," she mumbled. Why was he up there when the others had left? It occurred to her that he was much stronger than her and could likely tackle her out that door and over the parapet without anyone really noticing. Her throat constricted. If he really wanted her dead, this was his opportunity. "Sadly, I broke this vase. I hope Wilhelmina won't be disappointed."

With a tense smile, she crouched down to pick up the pieces. Wolfgang stood for a while, then closed the roof access door. Without looking at him, Aldine noted every step he took. Her finger cut on the sharp piece of the vase, but she was too intently focused to worry about a little cut.

Heavy steps came forward and she stopped breathing. Was this where he acted against her? Grabbing the sharp piece that had sliced her, she held it in her hand in case her fears were realized. If she might not be able to fight his strength, she could mark him.

But his steps veered sideways to the internal door and he disappeared down the stairs.

A shuddering breath seeped out of her and she closed her eyes. Painful nervousness still ran through her blood and her hand shook as she continued to pick up pieces of the broken vase.

Chapter 23

DRAWING ANOTHER DEEP breath, Aldine looked down at the small, round table, still trying to get her nerves under control. Her mind was too jumbled to even consider what had just happened and what it meant. It was exhausting having to think and suspect every moment—every action and word. Someone was responsible and the talisman was driving them. That was where the problem stemmed from, so what was the point worrying about who it was acting through?

There was nothing up here that could represent the witches, and there was nothing below, so it had to be in the bedroom. It only left one option and it was time to deal with it. No more close calls with falling stone. No more feeling like someone was watching her all the time, waiting for an opportunity to strike.

Marching to the door, Aldine, closed it behind her. There was nothing up here for her, so she continued down and out of the house, ensuring she walked well away from the edge of the house, walking until she reached the outhouse were tools were stored.

Enough of sitting idly by and letting this encroach on her. It was time to act.

Searching through the machines, most of which looked fearsome with spikes and gears, she found what she was looking for along the far side of the wall. No, she would not meekly let this happen.

Taking it, she walked back to the house and by whatever mercy, no one came across her carrying an ax back to Heinrich's bedchamber. It was empty, which was lucky, because she had no excuse in mind for what was just about to happen.

Swinging it with all her might, it bit into the dark wood of the bedframe. The strike reverberated up her arm, even as she pulled it free and struck again. The hits left ugly splinters and she kept striking, into the carved headboard, then one of the pillars. Even the mattress and bedsheets.

Where her strength came from, she didn't know, but she kept striking.

"What are you doing!?" Heinrich roared from the door before he came to wrestle the ax from her hands. She refused to let go, feeling she wasn't done yet. Was it enough to destroy the talisman? It had to be the bed.

Forcefully, he wrenched the ax from her hands.

"It's the bed. Don't you see that?"

He stared at her like she was completely incomprehensible, then pulled his gaze away and surveyed her damage. "You've lost your mind."

"It's a talisman," she said, pointing at the bed. "The curse is imbued in the bed."

"Your nerves have gotten the better of you."

"It's not my nerves," she bit harshly. "This bed is cursed, but for some reason you refuse to see that. Perhaps because it doesn't affect you."

"What are you talking about?" he said incredulously. "This is utter nonsense."

"Except everyone who marries you ends up dying, and now it's trying to kill me. I see these things in my dreams, and you don't believe me. This horrid house is cursed. This bed is cursed, and all you do is accuse me of being fanciful. Did I imagine that stone a hair's breadth away from my head? Was that my imagination too?"

"It was an accident."

"Well, a lot of accidents seem to happen around here, and all you do is ignore it and tell me it's not happening, that what I am experiencing is all in my head. Something is trying to kill me and all you can do is drug me so I haven't even got any vestiges of defense against this. That is what I see." Everything was just flowing out of her and she was unable to hold it back.

Heinrich remained silent and Aldine tried to calm herself. Her whole body was shaking.

"The Tober woman said—"

"That woman is mad."

"—said there was a talisman close to where all the activity was happening. And this is where it happens," she said, pointing at the bed. "Break the talisman and the curse ends."

With his hands on his hips, he stared at her. Then he softened. "Come here," he finally said, stepping closer and putting his arms around her. Aldine's body still felt like it was fighting, so it was hard to simply accept the calm embrace. It also made it hard to fight the tears. All the nervous tension she'd felt building up, released out of her and she sobbed. Hot, angry tears seeped out of her eyes and onto the soft cotton of his shirt.

"You know I don't believe in curses, but you do," he said. "I'm sorry this has been so distressing for you."

Softly stroking her hair, he held her.

"I did not imagine that stone," she said.

"No," he agreed. Surprisingly, he didn't make excuses like the wind had moved the heavy stone and ultimately toppled it just as she had been walking past. It was the first time he hadn't dismissed any of this as simply her fanciful imagination. "If it makes you feel better to destroy this bed, if you feel like it is the source of some malaise, then destroy it. It has never been my intent to make you feel uncomfortable."

She didn't move, because it was so lovely just to be held. There had been such a distance between them, she hadn't felt anyone in this house being on her side, least of all him.

"And I am sorry about the doctor. I honestly thought it would calm your nerves."

"My nerves are not the issue. I don't have problems with my nerves. At least not before coming here. There is something in this house."

"And destroying this bed will fix that?"

"Apparently."

"What's going on?" Ludwig said from the door. Aldine could feel hand gestures behind her. Right now, feeling so raw, she didn't want to deal with Ludwig and Heinrich sent him away.

They stayed like that for a while longer.

"I will build you a new bed," he finally said. "I am not much of a carver, but I can make you a new bed."

Aldine's eyes and nose felt raw and hot with the tears she had shed, but they were drying up now. Heinrich let go of her, and went over to the bed, pulling one of the pillars until it fell away from the rest of the bed. "We can even burn it if you like."

"I know you don't believe me," she said.

"I don't know what to believe anymore. Whatever I do, I can't seem to fix anything. You are wrong when you say this doesn't affect me. As hard as I try to keep everything together, I can't seem to make things right. It always goes wrong—disastrously wrong. I have ignored you. I didn't mean to, but there have been some heavy blows, and perhaps when things started going sideways again, I... "

"You distanced yourself," she finished for him.

"I didn't mean to. I didn't intend to be cruel. It just seemed that my bad luck never ends." He took her hand in his. "For a while, it seemed like that was all in the past, those misfortunes I had the ill luck to suffer, but you became increasingly unhappy. I just want a normal, contented marriage, but forever things seem to go wrong. Maybe God has cursed me. Or witches, as you believe. At this point, I am desperate enough to believe anything. I don't want to lose you too, so if burning this bed will put an end to all this, then I'll help you do it."

Moving closer, Aldine walked into another embrace. "I hope so," she said.

"If it could only be that easy," he said, putting his arms around her again. "I am sorry if you ever felt that I wasn't standing by you. That was never true. I just..." he drifted off. "I just want all to be well."

Aldine felt the barriers that had been between them dissipate. At least she hoped so. This house was a cold, harsh place without an ally.

"Come on, then," he said, pulling away from her. "Let's build a pyre and burn this to cinder."

"We can sleep in my room for a while," she suggested, but Heinrich was distracted by tearing one of the side boards away, forcing a crunching sound as the attachments splintered. Taking it on his shoulder, he carried it out of the room.

This felt like hope. It felt good. They were doing this together, a statement that they both wanted a happy future together. A weight was coming off her shoulders. This was bringing them together, and she understood more of his intentions, and the worry that had driven him to distance himself.

Grabbing one of the pillars, she lifted it. It was heavy, but she was not weak. She certainly wasn't going to meekly succumb to anyone—let alone long-dead witches.

Chapter 24

"THIS IS MADNESS," Ludwig stated, approaching Heinrich as he stood on the lawn and poured oil on the remnants of his bed. "That bed is centuries old. It is an heirloom of this house, of this family. It is not your place to burn it simply because your mad bride wants you to."

"If burning this bed will serve my bride, then I will do it," Heinrich stated.

"And what's next? What else will we have to sacrifice to the altar of her insanity?"

Aldine had never heard him speak like this—certainly not this animatedly about anything. She also hadn't understood this was what he thought about her. Cordiality in everything was what he'd shown her—until now.

"She belongs in a sanitorium. You need to send her away."

"She didn't imagine the stone falling on her," Heinrich replied.

"A mere happenstance, but from there she builds fanciful castles in the air. She's mad," he said, pointing sharply to his head with his forefinger. "Are we all to dance attendance to her superstitions and paranoia? Shall we burn all our furniture?"

"Ludwig," Wilhelmina said calmingly.

"What? You believe this? You believe we should burn our things to appease her?"

Wilhelmina didn't utter what she truly believed.

Everyone had been attracted by this commotion, standing around the fire that now roared up as Heinrich threw a match on the oil-soaked wood. They were all distracted by the fire for a moment.

If the ax hadn't destroyed the talisman, then this certainly would. Aldine felt relief. Not simply because this curse was broken, but that she and Heinrich were united. Even if he didn't truly believe, the fact that he would do this for her meant a great deal.

"Shall you sleep on the floor like animals?" Elke asked.

"I own a timber mill. I can damned well build my wife a bed," Heinrich replied.

Ludwig snorted with disgust. Wolfgang said nothing—only stared at the fire. He ventured no opinion. Wilhelmina remained quiet as well.

"Keep this up and the crazy wench will probably end up burning the whole house down," Ludwig muttered.

"Shut up!" Heinrich yelled. "That is my wife and you will show her due respect. Never forget who it is you're speaking about."

"Boys!" Wilhelmina chided. "This is helping no one. We must all respect one another."

Aldine pressed her lips together, because respect wasn't always a virtue Wilhelmina prescribed to—other than with her two sons. As for the rest of them, they all suffered from her disdain at times. Especially Wolfgang.

"Now if we are done with this," Wilhelmina said sharply, "our supper is getting cold. I for one, have had enough of peculiarities today." Her voice broke a little. It had been a strenuous day for all of them.

With a sharp turn, Wilhelmina marched back to the house, her back ramrod straight. Ludwig followed, taking Elke along with him.

Wolfgang stayed for a moment, his attention still captured by the fire. "It was a ridiculous and ugly bed anyway," he finally said before stepping away and walking into the darkness.

"He's not much for ornateness," Heinrich said. He always defended Wolfgang, no matter how uncouth he spoke. Aldine expected that Heinrich showed loyalty specifically because Wolfgang was so thorny. He was a kind and loyal brother. "He didn't mean it." Heinrich said, looking at her.

"About the bed?"

"Ludwig. He just..."

Heinrich defended him too—was always the peacemaker in the family. A role that was probably necessary to hold them all together. Aldine had never thought about it before, and she was proud of him for it.

"Overwrought?" she offered a little sarcastically.

Heinrich smiled. "Yes, that too."

"It's been a trying day for everyone."

Walking over, he leant down to kiss her and she smiled as she received it. It felt like they were a team now, husband and wife. The kiss was sweet and light.

"Come, let's eat," he finally said when they broke apart. Taking her hand, he led her back to the house.

Weber was serving by the time they walked into the dining room. Everyone was tense and uncomfortable that night, except Aldine. Tonight, she had her husband fully on her side, and that was the most wonderful feeling in the world. They held hands all the way to the point where they sat down. Supper was a quick affair, and afterward, when the others were going to the salon for drinks, Aldine excused herself, saying she needed to go make preparations. They were moving from his bedroom to hers, after all.

The fire had not been lit in his room as the cooler evening air descended. It seemed the servants had anticipated the move. Heinrich's room was in darkness and it looked empty and forlorn without the bed.

Grabbing a lantern, Aldine walked in. The servants had moved Heinrich's toiletries as well, but the ax was still there, standing upright against the wall.

This room had been the center of her fears and hopes. Now she only felt hope. This had been a decisive move and they had won. The bed was destroyed and the witches' power dealt to.

Walking over to the window, she saw her own reflection in the glass of the dark windows before closing the shutters. She wasn't sure why she did it, but it felt right. Perhaps they would vacate this room for a while. Changing rooms felt a little like a new start and that pleased her.

With the shutters secure, she walked back toward the door, but stopped. Hairs rose along the back of her neck, because she felt a current of heat. Nothing near what she felt during the nights when she woke, but there was a distinct wave of heat. She knew what it felt like—like a fire turning in the wind, but there was neither wind nor fire. How could that be? The bed was destroyed.

Lifting the lantern, she searched. There was nothing on the floor. Nothing that could have fallen from the bed. No remnants she could see. It had all been burnt, every last inch of it.

As the shadows of her lantern shifted, they fell on the painting. Aldine moved closer to the familiar scene of people sitting in a hall, or a courtroom. She'd looked at this painting countless times. Spotting something, she looked closer, bringing the lantern up to the canvas.

Through the window of the hall in the painting, she saw a pyre with a woman burning. It was only small, drawn with clumsy strokes. It had never been there before tonight.

"No, you don't," Aldine said harshly and turned back for the ax.

Returning with the blade, she cut through the canvas where the pyre was, the material curling with the release of tension. Dropping the ax, she tore the rest of the canvas, ripping it out of the frame. She even held pieces of it to the flame in her lantern.

If it had been the painting all along or if the witches' curse had jumped from the bed to the painting, she didn't know, but she wasn't going to let them. Even the frame she took down and broke, before opening the shutters and the window and throwing the pieces into the darkness.

Witches were not going to bother this house again, even if she had to vigilantly guard against giving them entry into the house again. It didn't matter if Heinrich didn't truly believe her—or anyone else for that matter. Those hags would not come into this house again. If she had to become the expert in fighting witches, she would.

Standing with her arms crossed, she looked out the window. It occurred to her that she had become the witch hunter in the house of witch hunters. Even so, she could not condone what had been done to these women back in those days, but she was not letting their curse poison the present, or the future—poison their children.

Closing the shutters firmly, she turned her back and walked out the door, shutting the door behind her. Putting the lantern on the hall table, she walked downstairs, feeling very calm and even empowered. She had won this fight and now she was going to have a nice evening with her husband.

Perhaps now they could build the bond between them that had been interrupted with all this. This new sense of purpose and empowerment also left her feeling better able to deal with Heinrich's family—and all their peculiarities. Saying that, she was still angry with Ludwig for outright calling her mad. Some true colors had been revealed tonight and although she might forgive, she wasn't sure she would forget.

Chapter 25

IT WAS THE FIRST TRULY peaceful night Aldine had had in this house, waking in her room with the sun gently shining in. Heinrich was dressing and getting ready for the day, and she sat up in bed and simply watched him.

"What?" he asked, looking over at her as he pulled on his jacket.

"Nothing," she said with a smile.

"Do not tempt me."

She hadn't been aware that she was. For once she was actually wearing her nightgown in the morning, not been forced to peel it off sometime during the night. "Where will you go today?"

"The mill," he said. "We are harvesting at the moment. Wolfgang will set off for Munich in the afternoon with a consignment of lumber."

"Then I wish him an uneventful journey."

With a nod, he left the room and quietly closed the door behind him. It was strange having him in her room, where he normally never went. It made her a little self-conscious of her things.

Anna came shortly after he left and lit the fire, which crackled gently. The mornings were still a little chilly, even as the days warmed nicely.

As soon as the worst of the chill was gone, Aldine rose and dressed with Anna's help. Breakfast was soon to be served and she walked downstairs as it started.

Wilhelmina and Elke were both sitting in the dining room, both quiet as she entered. Well, the peace she had found between herself and her husband didn't extend to her in-laws, who seemed very uncomfortable in her presence. "Good morning," she said brightly.

"Yes," Wilhelmina said and Elke simply stopped chewing and watched the scene. "Excuse me," the older woman uttered and walked from the room.

"It was certainly an interesting evening last night, wasn't it?" Elke said, continuing to eat. She waited for a response, but Aldine couldn't really think of anything to say as her husband had blatantly accused her of being mad. What did one say to such a thing? "Ludwig was a little disturbed by the scene, I think."

"I suppose it was quite a scene," Aldine admitted.

"Can't say I understand what happened, but you seem quite serene today."

"A good night's sleep is always refreshing." If Elke understood the subtext, Aldine didn't know, but it had been a badly needed night of sleep.

"Then let's pray for calm. Such dramatics are disconcerting for the soul, or have you any more rituals to exorcise spirits from the house?"

"No, I believe it is quite done."

"Excellent," Elke smiled. "Perhaps we should not mention this to Reverend Stubbe. He would look down upon such things. I think I will work on my embroidery this morning. What are your plans?"

Elke was being polite and keeping her company while she ate, and Aldine did have an appetite that morning. The release of nervous tension brought back her pleasure in food. Still, though, so not to take up too much of Elke's time, she ate quickly, to then join Elke in the salon.

For a while, Aldine read while Elke worked on their embroidery. The silence was comfortable between them.

Wilhelmina joined them for lunch and the silence continued, but more piercingly. It was an entirely different level of discomfort, but it was much easier to bear without constantly thinking someone or something was trying to kill her. Aldine accepted that there was some aftermath from the activities of destroying the talisman. That was fine. They would calm in a few days when they realized she wasn't about to run through the house raving.

Heinrich came shortly after three in a cart with wooden planks on the back. As soon as she saw him, Aldine walked outside to meet him, feeling comfortable for the first time since he'd left that morning. That was as it should be, though, shouldn't it? That seeing her husband was a pleasure.

"Oak," he said as he jumped off the cart. Several thick planks were stacked in the back.

"For our bed," she realized as he started picking them up one by one and carrying them into one of the outhouses that had a space for work.

"Yes, our new bed. I like oak. It is a nice color." It was certainly more cheery than the almost black of the bed that had been. "A simpler design."

"I agree," Aldine said. "Can I help?"

Heinrich left and returned with another plank. "If you wish. It is hard work."

"I don't mind work. I will take it over embroidery any day."

"You say that now. Wait until we get started. Have you ever used a planer before?"

"No, but I have seen one used."

"Well, then, you can start on this one. All the rough edges need to be planed down."

"I can do that."

The planer was a wooden block with a blade cut into the bottom of it. It was harder to use than she'd expected, needing some force to draw across the wood, but she didn't mind. It was enjoyable just to be here with him, working together. They worked in silence, and she much preferred to be out here spending time with him than in the salon.

"You're beautiful when you're concentrating," Heinrich said after a while, breaking into Aldine's focus.

"You working is not exactly a painful sight either."

He seemed pleased with the compliment, because he moved closer. A small thrill spiraled through her as he gently stroked down her cheek with the back of his forefinger. His eyes lingered on her lips and the thrill turned into something more heated.

Leaning down, he kissed her, a slow, lingering kiss. Soft lips pressed to hers and she lost herself in it. This was more playful, softer than the things they did in the dark. She didn't mind those things, but this was lighter, as if there were no expectations behind it. It was just him and her, enjoying being together. In fact, she wasn't sure he had kissed her, properly kissed her, during the day before.

Her breath echoed off the brick walls inside their workroom. Goosebumps had risen along her flesh from the soft touches between their bodies. Her lips felt like they were on fire and she needed him to quench the thirst.

With firm hands at her hips, he lifted her up and set her down on the wooden plank that ran between two stands. It gave slightly with her weight, putting their lips right in line and the kiss lingered. He toyed with her tongue, nibbled at her lips, teased along that most sensitive part along her lips.

"We're not going to get much work done like this," she said breathily.

"We have all the time in the world."

It was a lovely thought. There was no rush; there was nothing more important than playing and teasing—wanting each other. Burning heat inside her proved how much she wanted him. This desire she felt for him was something she hadn't expected, since their marriage had been an arrangement rather than a love match.

Warm hands stroked up her thighs under her skirts, slowly advancing. Aldine held her breath as the sensation grew more intimate and heady. His slow, even breathing flared on her cheek, but she felt his desire. Her own breath was constricted by her dress, which strained against her aching nipples, every breath teasing them further. "Heinrich," she said, unable to take much more of the tension that was forming inside her.

Hard fingers teased her through the soft cotton of her undergarments and she parted her thighs for him, giving him further access to her. It felt wanton; it was wanton, but right now, she wanted him with such force, she didn't know what to do with it.

His fingers pressing on her entrance made her groan, her back arching into the pleasure it rendered. There was nothing wrong with a wife wanting her husband so wantonly, was there? Each stroke had more moans escaping her throat, but he never rushed, his deft fingers teasing her at a mercilessly slow pace.

Slipping inside her garments, his fingers pressed inside her, the sensation flowered further and her head sank back, enslaved to the relentless sensation that was radiating out to every part of her body.

She didn't even feel the strings that held her undergarments give way, but she felt his fingers being replaced by the larger and firmer part of him, her body yielding as he pressed inside her. A fullness that felt so right, so lovely. The tension built a feverish edge and she needed more.

Fully enveloped, he ground into her, still at the same merciless pace. In the stillness, every contraction inside her was distinct and strong, wanting him deeper and firmer. "Heinrich," she pleaded, unable to take the strain anymore.

He ground into her harder, bringing the rush that built into a surge. It took her very consciousness with it, losing her in blissful pleasure as his groans echoed through her ears.

Heavens that they could do this. It was too good to be allowed. There had to be sin in something that was this tempting, this exquisite.

"Already we have christened this bed and it's not even built yet," he said, his breath harsh and striving. "This will definitely be our marriage bed and we will savor it every night."

"Yes," she said, smiling through her languid satedness. Every strength in her had just left her, but she didn't regret it for a moment.

Chapter 26

HEINRICH HELPED ALDINE out of the carriage as they returned from Sunday service with Reverend Stubbe. A mere week ago, Aldine had been a tense bundle of nerves sitting in the family pew and wondering what she was going to do about otherworldly things pressing in on her life. Now she felt like she was back to normal. Everything was right in the world, and she felt assured the world of spirits and superstition was something she could put behind her.

Wilhelmina and Elke walked into the house before her, but Aldine preferred to stay with Heinrich, who had been perfectly attentive to her. They were just about to have luncheon and even Wolfgang was joining them today, which was unusual. Normally he disappeared somewhere on Sunday, but not today.

No doubt Wilhelmina was overjoyed about this. Elke was probably not too pleased either, but Aldine still didn't know why they didn't like him. If it had been Wolfgang the curse had been acting through, it wasn't his fault. But their dislike could not be based on that or they would have said. It was something else. It wasn't any of her affair, she decided.

Ludwig was solemn and decidedly ignoring her. Clearly he hadn't forgiven the burning of the bed, but where did his anger stem from? Was it him the curse had been acting through?

Stop it, she told herself. There was no point rehashing something that was over and done with. It was time to focus on the future and to forget the past. Ludwig would come around eventually. The important part was that the relationship between her and her husband was better than it ever had been. The distance that had existed between them had gone. It had been driven by his fear of further tragedy.

But she had been strong; she had defeated the curse and emerged victorious. Hopefully now, they would simply be happy, and children would come. At times, her stomach felt ill and she wondered if it was a sign that a child had taken root inside her. As of yet, there had been no confirmation.

Sighing deeply, she pulled herself out of her thoughts and looked around the table. The food smelled delicious, cold pork that had been braised in the oven for several hours early that morning. She could almost feel how tender it was before taking a bite.

"We are to visit Lady Thainer," Wilhelmina said in response to a question. "She asked us to call. But I think it is better you stay at home, Aldine, and... recover from your ordeal."

Aldine frowned slightly before smiling. They were excluding her, which was fine. She had no particular desire to spend the afternoon with Lady Thainer. "Of course," she said, realizing that they were worried about what she would say and do, perhaps reveal how she had been tearing through the house trying to find talismans to break. They clearly didn't trust her to act reasonably in front of this woman whom Wilhelmina wanted to make a good impression with.

The luncheon finished and they retreated to the salon for a little while. Heinrich was first to leave, saying he wanted to work on the bed. Luckily Reverend Stubbe wasn't coming to visit, because he would frown on any work being done on Sunday. Ludwig saw Wilhelmina and Elke out to the carriage as he had promised to drive them over to Lady Thainer's manor. Aldine wasn't sure that Elke wanted to go as much as she was required to go. Lady Thainer hadn't exactly treated her as a valuable guest last time. Her station as the wife of the second son obviously didn't put her in high esteem with the lady.

Elke had never mentioned a word of the treatment, but it was unjust. It was a reason Aldine didn't enjoy Lady Thainer's company to the degree Wilhelmina did.

And then the house was empty. Everyone had gone their separate ways and she was left to see to herself. In a way, it was a relief as there were no judging observation constantly trying to spot anything wrong with what she did and said. It was just her, and she could enjoy finishing her tea in calm silence.

The ticking of the clock was all that was heard, the bird chirped outside. It was actually quite a lovely house once away from the family relationships and power struggles. For a moment, she indulged in imagining what it would be like if only herself and Heinrich lived here. It was an indulgence that was never to be. Heinrich liked his family around him. Perhaps when children came, it would urge Ludwig to move out. Nothing had ever been mentioned in that direction. The house was large enough to accommodate everyone.

With nothing to do and no one to talk to, Aldine fell asleep, the slow steady ticking of the clock carrying her away. Her dreams were colorful. She dreamt of animals and the forest, but it was almost as if they had been drawn for a child's fairy tale. There was nothing sinister about them, but they were unusually vivid.

Aldine woke with a start in the salon where she had fallen asleep in a chair. She frowned, not liking anything being unusual. Just a strange dream, she told herself. At least colorful dreams of animals were better than other dreams she'd had in this house.

Picking up her book, she started to read again, but her mind drifted off and she caught herself reading the same sentence over and over again. Perhaps she needed to recover from the tension and exertion from the last few weeks. At times she had been utterly terrified and that was bound to take a toll.

Putting the book down, she gave up. Reading just wasn't on the cards for that day. Her teacup was next to her and she picked it up, but the brew was cold, so she replaced it. "Weber," she called and rose from her chair. The manservant didn't respond so she called again, before remembering that it was Sunday and all the staff had the day off. There was no one to brew her a cup of coffee and the kitchen was somewhere she wasn't supposed to go, so she walked over to the teapot and poured some more into her cup. It was barely lukewarm, but it had to suffice.

Aldine didn't sit down again, feeling as if she'd been sitting for a long time. There was sunshine outside, but the grass drew her attention. Its greenness was so bright it almost glowed. Perhaps the sun was growing stronger. The hour bell chimed, which was funny. It had chimed mere minutes ago. Something had to be wrong with the clock.

The warmth of the tea had also dissipated completely. Perhaps she should sneak into the kitchen and make herself a pot of coffee, except she never managed to do a good job of it. Maybe Heinrich would like some.

Putting the teacup down, she decided she would venture into the kitchen. Her body felt sluggish as she moved as if walking through thick air. It was a strange notion. Thick air—who had ever heard of such a thing?

Hair rose along the back of her neck when she heard whispers. Despair descended on her. No, it couldn't be back. There couldn't be more of this curse.

Turning where she was, she tried to listen for where they came from. It had to be people outside talking, but the direction of the whispers wasn't from outside. They were from the wall. From the pictures.

As she stared at them, she saw the people in the pictures talking, saw them moving. They were just going about their business. One was selling parsnips to a wife carrying a wicker basket, while a man on a horse kept riding, even disappearing out of the picture.

With sheer astonishment and utter surprise, Aldine stared at them. They didn't speak clearly what they said, because they were talking to each other, not her. She didn't know what to do. This was madness. Pictures didn't move and talk. This was mad. Maybe it was her—she was mad and she had been all along.

Moving to the next pictures, she saw them moving too. A courtroom where the judge banged his gavel on the wooden bench, drawing attention back from something shocking that had been said. The woman in the witness box beseeched them pleadingly. Was that a witch being tried? This curse was still active.

A scream was trapped in her throat. This couldn't be. She had broken the talisman. Had they shifted to something else?

"Heinrich," she called with a growing sense of panic. Things were not alright. Just as she had started to believe everything was fine, everything was falling apart again. Every shadow was turning sinister, from every direction something sought to hurt her. "Heinrich!"

The whispers increased, burrowing into her thoughts, but there were too many for her to hear what any of them were saying.

Clasping her ears, she refused to hear them. This wasn't happening. They had been in the clear. They had been free, but now they were returning to utter madness. The façade of peace and veracity melting before her very eyes.

Chapter 27

ALDINE RAN OUT OF THE house and the brightness outside assaulted her eyes. Her body almost felt like it was floating, her limbs slow in doing what she wished them to. How could this be? What was going on? She was under attack somehow, but she didn't understand what was happening.

It felt almost as if she was out of her body, watching herself, while at the same time squinting from the painful brightness.

"Heinrich!" she called, seeing the grass come up to her face. It hadn't felt like she'd been falling, but now her head was on the grass, and she could hear the wind whisper through it.

This was danger. Danger was coming. From where she didn't know, but a panic had taken over her mind. Somehow she was being inundated and incapacitated.

An ant seemed to stop on a blade of grass and it turned its beady red head to her. "What are you doing on the grass?" it asked.

Scuttling herself back, she tried to get away from it. Was that the devil talking to her? Was it the witches teasing her? Ants did not speak.

Getting her body to move was hard. It was as if she had to learn to operate it. Move this leg, then the other. She fell to her knees, but she was on gravel now.

With determination, she walked toward the workshop where Heinrich was. It was a place of safety in this world that had turned upside down.

She called for him, but she wasn't entirely sure her mouth was working. Reaching for the end of the door, she grabbed it, relieved she had something to hold onto. It felt as if she was floating, as if the ground would not keep her down.

"Heinrich," she croaked and threw herself into the workshop. The planks were there, but Heinrich wasn't. Where was he? He was here; she knew he was here, but she couldn't see him. Were her eyes deceiving her?

A bird was staring at her, sitting on top of the edge of the door. It shook its wings and blue sparks came out. The noise of it was so loud it was deafening. Then the space in the yard out the door extended, making the house seem like it was much farther away. She was stranded in the workshop, knowing that she would fall if she stepped outside.

Deep terror bit into every part of her. She was going to die. She might be dying right now. The witches had finally struck and she was being pulled to pieces. Any minute now, her arms might tear off her. With all her strengths, she held onto them.

Behind her, the shadows were encroaching. They were coming for her, but if she walked outside, she would fall. A large hole was opening up, ready to swallow her. The wood beside her was producing rainbow patterns, coming apart in waves.

An anguished scream came and she wasn't sure where it had come from. Crouching down, she reached for the wall so she wouldn't fall. The rough of the wood seemed to pierce into her skin, but she refused to let go.

Steps like those of a giant echoed through her ears. Someone was coming. They were coming for her.

The shadow came across her, but she was too scared to look. Her breath too shallow to take in air. Her cheeks were wet and her throat was so dry she couldn't swallow.

Making herself look, she saw Wolfgang, but his face was distorted. He had horns. It was him. He was the devil. He'd been doing this to her all along.

Cowering, she turned her back on him. "No, no, no," she whimpered. He was here to hurt her. Talons touched her and she recoiled.

"Breathe," he said.

Breathe what? Was the air poisoned? Was it brimstone she would smell? No, she didn't want to breathe. He came closer and she screamed. With firm hands, he picked her up. The floor fell away and she was truly lost. She had lost her grip on the world and it was fleeting from her.

"No!" she screamed as he carried her out into the burning sun. The world had fallen away too, lost its consistency, and all she saw was color in the wildest patterns one could imagine. Did this mean she was dead? Was this death? "You will not get me. I will never concede."

Whispers around her, and she saw the scenes, the villagers moving, talking, laughing. Behind was a rushing sound as if she was standing inside a waterfall. They were in the house.

The blankets on her bed enveloped her, grabbing her, they refused to release her. What did this mean? She heard him walk, his steps on the floorboards and he sat down in the chair. She felt hate emanating from him. There were no features on his face, they had just melted away. He was just a shape over in the corner of the room.

The curtains of her bed appeared to be moving, pulsing like they had their own heartbeat. With cloying fear, her eyes darted between them and the figure of the devil, who hadn't moved from the chair across the room, not saying anything.

She tried to speak, but her throat was too constricted.

"Stop," she called, her hands to her ears, trying to block out all the whispers. All she wanted to do was run, but she couldn't. Her body refused to obey her. But luckily, the devil in the chair didn't come closer. At least there was that.

All she could do was to stare at the shifting colors on the ceiling. She couldn't move, couldn't think. There was no escaping.

Over time, the worst of the panic subsided a little. The pressing whispers were a little further removed, and she got more used to the idea that the world was not as it should be. It moved, shifted, undulated, tearing itself apart and putting itself back together in all sorts of strange ways.

Then she saw Heinrich appear above her. He was worried and the skin on his cheeks seemed to move as if he wasn't quite solid—liquid almost. A warm hand was comforting on her forehead. "Try to sleep," he said and she closed her eyes, but that only unleashed a complete lack of reality. It was better to keep her eyes open, even if the world was strange. It still had some familiarity.

Looking at the chair, the devil was gone. She tried to say something, but the words didn't come out. A moment later, Doctor Hagen was there, looking at her. She didn't like him—didn't trust him and she really didn't want him touching her.

He looked worried, kept calling her name, while she hoped he would go away if she ignored him. She certainly wasn't going to take any pills he wanted to shove down her throat. Perhaps he understood because he didn't give her any.

Her head ached, pounded relentlessly, but she refused to close her eyes. The craziness was less if she kept them open. Slowly, her body started to listen to her commands more. Although the touch of her own fingers to her face felt alien.

Heinrich returned into view once the doctor had gone. He urged her to drink something and cool wetness met her dry throat. But it didn't alleviate the deep tiredness she felt in both her body and mind. It was as if she had exhausted her reserve of fear and terror. Now she was only happy that the world was slowly becoming more stable.

"You should sleep," he said and she turned to her side. "The doctor thinks you have become affected by something."

She'd been affected by something almost from the day she'd arrived here. This was just its new strategy, and it was horrifying. This curse was becoming infinitely worse. The power of these witches meant they could infect her very life. This wasn't just dreams, but then it had been more than just dreams before, but nothing like this. It was as if they were releasing their full power. And she was an ant in a tempest, had no power whatsoever to combat them. How wrong she had been thinking she'd had victory over them. This she could not defeat, so was there any point in continuing? They had defeated her utterly.

Aldine couldn't answer. Her mind was too tired to even think about what he'd just said. Eventually, she couldn't stop herself from sleeping, where strange and wild dreams evolved around her. There seemed to be no message, just endless strangeness.

Even in her sleep, she knew she wanted to be away from this house. All the bad things were in this house, because she was here. All the hope they'd had on their honeymoon, away from everything. It had been sweet and sedate. Now all she had was fear and terror—and Heinrich. Their relationship was stronger, but at what cost? If she stayed here, they were going to kill her.

Chapter 28

SLUGGISH WAS PERHAPS the best way to explain how Aldine felt. The craziness had gone, but her head hurt and her stomach felt unsettled.

"How are you today?" Heinrich asked as he dressed.

"Better. Whatever attack it was, it has gone."

"You should stay in bed and recuperate. Doctor Hagen will be by later."

Trying to hide her dismay, she smiled weakly. The previous day had been the scariest experience of her life, and she still didn't know what to make of it. The world had literally gone to pieces. Then again, if Doctor Hagen stated that he thought she should go somewhere to recover, she would struggle to disagree. Being away from here had a strong appeal. It was difficult to say so to Heinrich, though. Part of her wanted to pack up and go home, but another part wanted to be with her husband. It was just this house. There was evil in this house.

"I better go. Take it easy today."

She nodded weakly.

They didn't speak of exactly what had happened. It was as if it was ignored and swept under the carpet. Truth was that Aldine had no idea what to do, how to stop this. Even now, she felt panic creeping up on her. The worst was that it had happened during the day, so there was no safe time. Before she had believed that she was at risk only at night time, but apparently, she was at risk at all times.

"She is insane," she heard a voice coming from below her window. It as Ludwig. She could tell by the voice.

"She had ingested something. Doctor Hagen said so," Heinrich said. He was defending her. Slowly, she moved closer to the window.

"She needs to be sent away. Who knows what she's capable of doing? You're not doing her a favor by keeping her here. She needs treatment by professionals."

"Can't you see that something is going on?" Heinrich shot back.

"Yes, we have a mentally unstable woman living in our house."

"My wife, you mean. And this is my house. If you don't like it, you can find somewhere else to go."

"You always were too sentimental and weak. And her obsession with fire. She will burn this house to the ground."

Frankly, it sounded like a good idea to Aldine. Maybe all of their problems would be solved if the house was destroyed.

"I am not sending her away. She was given something. Doctor Hagen—"

"That man is a quack, and he is only trying to please you so you keep paying him."

"I am not sending Aldine away. Something is happening in this house."

"She has infected you with her madness."

"This is enough of this talk. I will not hear of it. You are welcome to leave anytime you wish."

It warmed her heart that her husband defended her, that he believed her when she said something was very wrong here.

The brothers went their separate ways, neither of them happy. She could tell by his expression that Heinrich wasn't, but she suspected Ludwig was not done with his accusations. He believed that she was the source of all the problems in this house. Perhaps it was him that was her greatest enemy. He was certainly set against her, and increasingly so. If he had his way, she would be sent away to a madhouse and they would all continue as before—before she had come to the house. It did suggest that her presence had brought this all on, but that wasn't true. Josefina had experienced these things too. Although she could get little information about what the previous wife had gone through, suggestions were that nothing like Aldine had just experienced had ever happened to her.

*

As it got close to lunchtime, she dressed and went downstairs. The house was very quiet. Wilhelmina and Elke were there, but the men were gone, going about their usual business.

As expected her arrival was a muted affair, neither Wilhelmina nor Elke quite knew how to deal with her. Soup was served—onion and vegetables. Aldine was actually grateful it wasn't a rich flavor.

"I say this as a friend," Elke said, breaking the silence of the room, "but perhaps Ludwig is right and you would be much happier being tended to by professionals who know how to deal with this kind of hysteria."

Aldine didn't know how to respond. Neither did Wilhelmina apparently, who made disapproving noises at the direct statement.

"I don't suffer from hysteria," Aldine said quietly and Elke raised her eyebrows as if dealing with someone completely delusional.

"Of course you don't," she said lightly and patted Aldine's hand. "It's just that you seem very unhappy here. It's just an option you should consider. Doctor Hagan will likely say something similar when he comes. I understand he is arriving shortly. But never mind. I thought we all needed a bit cheering after all the dramatics. I asked the cook to prepare a strudel for us this afternoon. It always picks me up when I am feeling things pressing on me. I know you said you missed the patisseries in Manheim. Sugar is good for shock, they say. Puts everything to right, you'll see."

That was very kind and Aldine smiled at the consideration.

Doctor Hagen arrived shortly after lunch and he tended to her in the salon. Wilhelmina and Elke were both present.

"How do you feel?" he asked.

"Better. A headache, but my stomach feels better after eating."

"Good, good," he said absently. "No more hallucinations?"

"No, everything is fine today."

He proceeded to check her eyes, her tongue and even the sides of her neck. "I worry that you ingested something that didn't agree with you."

Listening, Aldine tried to think what it would be. "I didn't eat or drink anything that the others did not." Thinking back, that was true. There was nothing she had eaten uniquely.

"Well, different people have different reactions to things. One can suffer from allergies very strongly while the next person feels nothing."

"So that is what you think it was?" Wilhelmina asked. "An allergic reaction?"

Doctor Hagen looked at her carefully. "It could be." He turned his attention back to Aldine. "You have not taken anything that someone has given to you, like that women in Gelling Forest?"

Wolfgang must have revealed that she had seen her.

"No, she gave me nothing."

"Then why would you go see someone like that?" Wilhelmina demanded, clearly distressed by this revelation.

Aldine didn't know what to say for a moment. She couldn't very well reveal in front of Doctor Hagen that she had gone to gather information about breaking witch curses. He would cart her off to a madhouse immediately. "I just thought I would find out about medicinal herbs, but she didn't give me any, and I haven't taken any."

Doctor Hagen did not look convinced. "There are things in nature that can be very dangerous. They are not to be toyed with."

"I understand," Aldine said, knowing it sounded as though she had accidentally done this to herself.

With that, the doctor stood up and prepared to leave. "Just be very careful," he said and she nodded, knowing he was admonishing her and assuming that because she had gone to see Mrs. Tober, she was doing something she shouldn't.

The disapproval emanating from Wilhelmina was even worse now than Aldine had thought possible.

"Time for strudel," Elke said brightly and got up to go speak to Weber.

Wilhelmina remained utterly silent and refused to look at her. There was no point explaining to the woman that this was not her doing, that she had not done this to herself. It wouldn't be believed.

Elke returned holding a pot of tea.

"I might pass," Aldine said. "In case it is the mint tea that affects me."

"Mint has never interfered with anyone, but if you insist," she said, pouring herself a cup and taking a sip. "Would you like some, Wilhelmina?"

"No, thank you."

"Wilhelmina does not like strong flavors. Ah, and here comes the strudel," she said as Weber came into the room, carrying a tray. "I will serve," she said as he put it down and reached for the knife to cut into the crisp pastry with icing sugar sprinkled on top. The smell of apples filled the room. "I do love raisins, they always remind me of childhood. All good things have raisins, don't they?"

Portions were positioned on plates and Elke handed them out. "I would say I am surprised that Wolfgang took you to see that woman, but it really isn't a surprise, is it? Trust him to consort with a woman like that."

"He didn't—" Aldine started.

"He hates women, you know. Always has. Even his mother. Blames her for his misfortune and reduced circumstances in life. Was quite awful to her from what I hear."

Perhaps Aldine was finally hearing Elke's objection to the man. Wilhelmina snorted dismissively, but Aldine didn't know if that was in agreement with his despicable character or that Elke was mentioning it.

"He'll never marry, of course. Who would want to marry him? Has no prospects other than his brother's generosity. What woman would hitch their wagon to that? No one is more jealous of the title. Being the oldest, he firmly believes it should be his. You should hear him speak once he's had a few drinks. The things he says in the village would shock you. I've told Ludwig again and again, but he is completely blinded. Wolfgang positively toys with their loyalty, plays with their guilt."

"Guilt?" Wilhelmina shot in. "Guilt for what? Always was a sniveling little gutter rat," Wilhelmina continued, revealing a harsh resentment beyond anything she had mentioned before. "Always trying to push into the family, wanting attention for the smallest little thing."

That seemed a bit harsh. "He was a child."

"Well, a child should know his place," the older woman bit back.

Elke sighed. "Always leads to trouble when someone has ambition beyond their means. It is cruel of his brothers to encourage him, but they will not listen to us, will they, Wilhelmina? They will learn one day, mark my words. That man engages in every vice there is. Positively hated Luise, didn't he, Wilhelmina?"

"Yes," the woman replied. "Didn't much care for her."

"Didn't think much better of Josefina either, who was a lovely girl. Oh, and who wants vanilla sauce? I ordered some vanilla and it finally arrived. I simply adore the taste. Aldine?"

"Please," she said and Elke poured the pale yellow sauce across her portion of strudel, the little specs of vanilla visible.

"One must have one's little luxuries every now and then. Wilhelmina?"

"No, thank you," the woman said, accepting her plate.

Pouring a little on her own plate, Elke took it and cut into the strudel. The taste exploded in Aldine's mouth. It did remind her of home. They had some lovely patisseries where one could take some coffee and a slice of cake during an afternoon, particularly in summer. The taste of strudel and vanilla brought back so many memories. This was a lovely addition to the day, even if these revelations about Wolfgang were disturbing.

Chapter 29

"IT IS A BIT STIFLING IN the house," Elke said as she walked outside. "Wilhelmina is in a mood. I don't think you are her favorite."

"No," Aldine agreed. From the start, she had never been Wilhelmina's favorite, and even less so now. With a sigh, Aldine wrapped her shawl more tightly around her and kept walking.

"Come autumn, the harvest season starts. It's the busiest time of the year," Elke went on. "I know this meadow where there are wild roses. I know you like to draw flowers. It's not far. The most iridescent pink. I'm not sure you will be able to depict them as they are. It must be an impossible color to achieve with paint."

"I can always try." It would be nice to get back to drawing, to the person she had been before all this worry had claimed her. The truth was that she didn't know what to do and was feeling a little as if she was losing herself. During the day, she had wondered about asking Heinrich if she could go visit her family. It was highly unusual so early in a marriage, but with all these developments, she could use a respite and a chance to regain herself.

"Some flowers on the wall would certainly be nicer than those awful paintings that are there now. They just refuse to change things around the house. Why is that, do you think?"

"I don't know." It wasn't something that had occurred to her.

"It's so old-fashioned. We should really tear the house down and build something modern—but they won't hear of it. They hold onto the past."

The family didn't really talk about the past or the role they had played in it other than that they were an old, established family in the district.

They quickly walked along a path Aldine hadn't seen before. It was a direction she had never taken before now. The weather was perfect for a walk, cool, but not cold. The sun shone, creating patterns on the ground through the leaves. The birds chirped.

"Your father would never approve of such an old building," Elke continued.

"Well, he does appreciate architecture from all eras. They represent the values of the time—functional versus decorative. They are virtues that shift over time." She was starting to sound like one of her father's lectures and a pang of longing for her old life hit her—a life devoid of uncertainty and fear. Now she seemed to live with both—unsure what people thought of her and that they would turn on her. What she truly feared was that Heinrich would turn on her, but he had shown himself steadfast. That was worth fighting for.

"I do like modern architecture—light and airy, instead of just dark and somber. It could not have been fun living in those times. Don't you think?"

"Not if they were going around burning anyone with an opinion," Aldine said unguardedly.

"Exactly," Elke said with a smile. "Anyone with ambition, with drive. They are always attacked." Was she talking about Wolfgang? She had just now accused him of those very things, although Aldine herself had never observed this ambition Elke was speaking of. He was rude and abrupt, but she had never observed the harsh character that Elke and Wilhelmina obviously saw.

"I suppose that is true."

"The world has always hated women with drive. Still do."

Aldine wasn't entirely sure where Elke was going with this conversation.

"Be demure, accept everyone's opinion around you and never act for yourself."

"Well, I'm not sure—"

"Just accept what everyone wishes to do to you, and never insist on what you truly deserve."

Confused, Aldine didn't understand what Elke was referring to. Maybe Wilhelmina, who had fairly strict views on what women should be and do. Elke had been subject to those opinions for quite a while. "No one can decide the things you are passionate about for you. You simply are, or you are not."

Elke stopped walking. "Not everyone is strong. And not everyone sees strength."

"What do you mean?"

"Nothing," she said after a moment. "How are you? You look a bit flushed?"

"Do I?"

"Are the witches coming for you?"

"What?"

Elke's smile didn't falter and Aldine could only stare at her. "They're coming, you know. They're going to get you."

Taking a step back, Aldine's hand went to her neck. Something was wrong. Why was Elke speaking like this? The birds chirping was growing in sound, they squawked as if right by her ear, but she saw nothing. Something was very wrong. Elke only stared at her. It was her—it was her the witches were acting through. "You," Aldine said.

"Yes, me. Are you surprised?"

That distant, floating feeling descended on her as she turned to run. Her mind felt disconnected from her body, but she forced her limbs to move. The ground felt rubbery and soft under her feet, a sea of green around her, glowing like jewels.

"Not that way," Elke called behind her. "You'll never find your way back if you go that way."

The thought stuck in her mind, stoking the panic that had already gripped her. She would get lost if she went that way—lost in the forest where moss people were going to claim her.

"Heinrich," she called.

"Oh, he can't hear you, my dear. He doesn't believe you, you know. Thinks you're utterly mad. They all do. They're just humoring you, all the while planning to have you carted off to the madhouse. They're coming for you right now."

Changing directions, Aldine ran, but she lost the path and was floating on top of the forest floor, untied to a path and to safety.

"Not that way," Elke called. Aldine couldn't see her anymore. The trees seemed to be moving. Color emanated from them as they reached for her, trying to catch her.

A tug on her arm made her fall. "This way. Come on, walk you dozy cow. The witches want to meet you." Elke laughed.

"You're mad," Aldine managed to say.

"Am I? Do you really think so? Or is it witches coming for you? I can't help it. The witches make me do it."

"You gave something to me. The doctor said—"

"The doctor doesn't understand. No one understands."

An abyss opened up in front of her and it was far down to the ground. "No."

"Yes, I am afraid so," Elke said. "We just can't have you come along and messing things up."

Something in Aldine made her want to jump, to escape the dangers that were chasing her, but she had to think, had to separate the real from the panic. She had been poisoned in some way, a way that took her out of her mind.

"If Heinrich hadn't been so very stubborn, this wouldn't be necessary, but he always was too soft."

"Heinrich," Aldine repeated and she started to cry.

"This is his fault. If he'd only sent you away like he should have, this wouldn't be necessary."

"You killed the others," Aldine stated.

"No, the witches did," Elke laughed. "They know what is necessary."

Pushed and prodded, Aldine was losing her balance. Her fingers reached for something to hold, but everything she grabbed pulled away. Slowly, she was sliding into the abyss, prodded by Elke's foot. Aldine tried to grab the foot, but Elke shook her off.

Moss tore away in her hands as she scrabbled for safety. Elke was trying to kill her—that much she knew. Whatever she had been poisoned with, it was to incapacitate her, to make her stop fighting, but she fought with everything in her.

And then rushing, rock tore at her fingers and hands, her feet and her toes. She fell and hit and fell and hit. It wasn't pain she felt so much as shock. A branch hit into her stomach and for a moment, she thought her insides would burst out. Breathing was impossible, her lungs caught in a vice. Pain seared. Red took over her vision and the rocks whispered around her. It felt as if they moved to cushion her, but she knew that wasn't right. Rocks did not cushion, but at least they had stopped her fall. Above her, all she could see was red sky.

She heard crickets doing their song, ants marching and the leaves rustling above her head. She was no longer in her body; she was floating and she could see herself below, see the entire valley she had fallen into. The world was breaking apart into patterns and it was actually quite beautiful. Colors undulated into colors and as opposed to chasing her, it seemed they welcomed her, were putting on a show. And moss people, she saw them. Little bodies covered entirely with green moss. Large black eyes and tiny mouths. They surrounded her, but she didn't feel afraid.

They told her not to worry, that what was done was done, and there would be no more. They told her she could sleep now, that it was over. No witches descended; someone was protecting her from them, keeping them away from her. Maybe the moss people, maybe God. This beauty had to be God, didn't it? Because it was so beautiful, the world was like a giant jewel sparkling and shining, and peaceful. There was nothing to worry about now. Then all melted into darkness.

Chapter 30

IN THE BLACKNESS, she heard her name being called somewhere far in the distance, but she didn't want to answer. It was nice where she was, this blackness. There was nothing scary here and she could gladly stay. There would be badness if she left—somehow she knew that. Pain and badness.

Jarring scrapes pierced into Aldine's mind. She was still in darkness, but she knew it was close.

"Aldine." Fingers were touching her face—she could feel them. She didn't want to be drawn out of this comfort, but she was being drawn out whether she wanted to be or not. "We found you," he said. Heinrich, he had found her.

Sadness stole into her and she cried. Something awful had happened to her. She had thought she was dead, but she wasn't. Heinrich was here.

"Ludwig, we need something to carry her on," someone called loudly. Wolfgang.

"We've been looking for you," Heinrich said. "You had us worried."

Painful light pierced her eyes as she tried to open them. The colors were gone. The beauty was gone and all she saw was gray.

"We have to follow the stream downhill," Wolfgang said.

"Elke pushed me," Aldine said. "She pushed me off the cliff."

"You've hit your head. You don't know what you're saying." It was Heinrich and disappointed flooded her.

"I know exactly what happened."

"She said you had one of your attacks and ran off. She tried to stop you."

"She's lying," Aldine said, tears streaming from her eyes. They didn't believe her.

"We'll talk more about it later." Aldine didn't want to be dismissed and told to talk about it later. If they refused to believe her, she was going to quit this house and this marriage, she decided.

A stretcher made of a blanket and poles was being lowered and they grabbed her shoulders and legs to lift her on. Sharp pain released throughout her body and she screamed.

"Hush, hush," Heinrich said, stroking her hair. "You are injured, but you are alive. Your body is broken." He looked over at Wolfgang, who started lifting up the stretcher. There was no path down this valley, only wild rockiness.

"We'll come out along the Wyman bridge if we keep going down," Wolfgang said. "Better than going up. Ludwig will come with the cart."

Heinrich nodded and they started traversing the rough terrain, the stones at times shifting under their feet. It was a perilous descent, but Aldine wasn't sure her body—or her heart—could be more beaten. There was so much pain, she couldn't even identify where it was coming from. Every step was jarring, sending pain radiating through her body. She wanted to ask them to stop, but what was the point, the pain wouldn't stop and she would be pausing what had to happen anyway.

The descent down the valley was never-ending bumps and jars, endless pain. Finally she was being placed on the back of a cart, where the constant vibration and strikes of the wheel exacerbated every wound she had. Her leg was broken—that much she knew already. Her fingers were shredded and bloody.

Everyone came outside to meet them including Doctor Hagen, who had been summoned and had arrived in the time it had taken to carry her out of the awkward place she had fallen. Behind him, Wilhelmina stood, as did Elke.

"My poor dear," Elke said stepping forward. "What happened?"

So that was how she was going to play it, Aldine realized, deny she'd had any part in it.

"You just disappeared. I searched for you endlessly," the woman continued. "We are so glad you are safely returned to us. We were so worried."

Aldine couldn't believe the lies spewing out of the woman. Before she could say anything, she was carried into the house and up the stairs. Doctor Hagen fussed over her and finally gave her laudanum to dull the pain.

It made it hard to think as her mind was racing, trying to figure out how to deal with her enemy, an enemy that was trying to kill her. By the look of it, Elke certainly wasn't going to admit it, and most people, if not every person in this house, thought she was mad. Her mad episodes had been witnessed and Elke would use that as much as she could.

"You have a broken leg and a broken arm. The second is easy to set, the first is not. You must relax." Even with the laudanum, it was excruciatingly painful as he pulled on her broken limbs. It took time to set her bones properly, but the pain started to dull as the doctor went through the slow process of heavily bandaging her leg and arm.

Heinrich stayed with her, hovering in the background, ready to help should he be needed.

"Whatever I had ingested before," she said to the doctor, "I was given again, and then she dragged me to the cliff and pushed me over. Elke tried to kill me."

The doctor listened.

"Aldine," Heinrich said with exasperation.

"I might have been under the influence of whatever it was, but I still knew what was happening to me. I could still tell what she was doing."

"It is a grave accusation," Heinrich said.

"I know that," Aldine replied. "It was a grave thing to do."

"Then the police should deal with the matter." Doctor Hagan said.

"But he doesn't believe me," she said, indicating Heinrich.

"I never said that," Heinrich replied. "It's just..." The room was silent for a moment and finally Heinrich sighed.

"Elke will hang if the accusations are true," the doctor said.

"But she has killed two people already, and just tried to kill me," Aldine said.

"I am fairly certain a mind-altering substance has been used on the countess," Doctor Hagen said and it took a few seconds for Aldine to realize he was referring to her. The two men stared at each other for a while. Then he turned back. "With your leg and arm set, you can move around now, with the highest degree of care. Your spine appears unharmed which means you were very, very lucky. A fall like that. The angels were watching over you. The bruises will take some time to go, but you will recover with rest. I think you have a concussion too, but not a bad one.

"A branch slowed your descent," Heinrich said.

"Yes, very lucky," the doctor added. "Otherwise, there would not be this outcome. Now you must rest," he said, packing up his bag and putting on his coat.

Rest was what she needed; her body was beyond exhausted, but she was terrified of sleeping—terrified that Elke would sneak into her room and finish the work that had obviously failed. The women could be none too happy about this. "I don't think I dare sleep in this house," Aldine said.

"I will ensure no one disturbs you," Heinrich said.

"It's not 'disturbing' I worry about. She can't be happy I survived."

Heinrich bit his lips together. "It is a grave accusation," he repeated, "but I believe you, and believing you means I am culpable of letting her kill others too—under my very nose."

It was a perspective Aldine hadn't considered, but it was true.

"She taunted me," Aldine said. "Said the witches were coming for me. Her intent was for you to declare me insane so I would be carted off to a madhouse."

"Why, why would she do this?"

Shaking her head, Aldine admitted she didn't know. "If it is true she killed two of your brides already, then we can assume it has something to do with you marrying."

"Ludwig would know nothing of this," Heinrich said forcefully, again as if this was overwhelming him in its gravity. "Elke has been part of this family for close to four years. How could she do something like this? Why, why would she do something like this? If she wants the title and the estate, why not just kill me?"

"Because you would be much harder to kill and there would be suspicion cast on Ludwig. She could not use a witches' curse to torment you—you would not believe in such things. Too much could go wrong," Aldine said. "I don't know. My mind does not work the way hers does. In the forest, she talked about her ambition and drive, and why she should have the things she wanted."

"If she wanted her husband to have the title, then she would have to kill me."

"It could be next in her plan. Tormented by the loss of three brides, no one would challenge it if you appeared to do something unseemly."

Sharply, Heinrich rose. "I think we must deal with this. I will ask Anna to come sit with you and not let anyone into this room. We have a wheelchair somewhere. It was my father's. I will find it, but rest now."

Aldine didn't have to be convinced. Her eyes would barely stay open, even with pain starting to come back after the laudanum's effects started to taper.

Chapter 31

AS BRUISED AND BATTERED as she was, Aldine grew tired of lying in bed. She felt like a victim just lying there. Her leg was a nuisance, but the wheelchair provided her a means to sit and even be move if she wished. With her broken arm, there was little she could do for herself. Doctor Hagen returned the next morning and said it was fine for her to sit in the wheelchair, so she did. In some ways, she felt safer and more ready to defend herself if Elke came through the door.

"All you can do is mend," the man said. He was quite kind and he seemed to understand her distress, and even that she didn't wish to take any calming pills that made her less aware of her circumstances. It seemed the doctor believed her that this was being done to her, even if many were not convinced. Elke was probably downstairs right then, spinning her lies.

In fact, Doctor Hagen seemed reticent to leave, because he knew there was a real threat to her in the house. Anna also stayed in the room, but there wasn't much for her to do as Aldine wasn't dressing. So now, Aldine sat with a woolen blanket over her legs, her bandaged arm in a sling, making it hard to do anything other than sit.

What she really wanted to know was what was being done. Heinrich had said the police needed to be called for, but so far, they hadn't come. Granted, it would be a long way to the nearest police station. Out in such an isolated place, the community took care of their own needs. This might be beyond their capabilities however.

As she sat, raised voices floated up from downstairs. Well, they were definitely in discussions. It was a large house, so the discussion had to be fiery.

"I had better go see," Doctor Hagen said, who was the only person who could attest to substances being used on her. Quickly, he left the room. They were talking about her, about what had happened to her, and she wanted to be there.

"Anna, please wheel me to the landing," she ordered and the girl looked uncertain. "I need to hear what they say."

Reluctantly, the girl followed the command and the small, brass wheels of her chair squeaked as they rolled down the corridor.

"You cannot lay such accusations against my wife!" It was Ludwig speaking. "There is no proof, and these accusations come from your mad wife. She can hardly be acclaimed a believable witness with her witches' curses and pyromaniac habits."

"Aldine is not mad," Heinrich said. "Something—"

"Always something. Always some excuse. She needs to be carted away."

At the landing, Aldine could look down on them in the foyer below. Ludwig stood in front of Elke as if protecting her. Even Wolfgang was being drawn in from outside. Doctor Hagen stood at the bottom of the stairs.

"She simply ran away. What was I supposed to do? I can't help if she has a turn of insanity and runs off a cliff."

"A substance—" Doctor Hagen started.

"Oh, shut up," Ludwig bit in. "God knows what poisons that woman has been giving herself. She admitted going to see that quack in Gelling Forest."

"She didn't return with any substances," Wolfgang said.

"Oh please, women can hide whatever they want in their skirts," Elke replied tersely.

"But I did see you leave yesterday and dump these in the forest," Wolfgang said, pulling out a couple of pouches from his pockets.

"No, I didn't," Elke responded, but Doctor Hagen moved forward. Aldine couldn't see, so she sat up to see better over the banister. As she did, Elke looked up and Aldine saw pure hatred in her eyes. The mask was slipping, it seemed.

"Pennyroyal, and these are psilocybe. These are powerful hallucinogens," Doctor Hagen said, looking over at Elke. "The pennyroyal to ensure one does not conceive. Over time and at high dosages can induce fever and sweating. Even paralysis and death at high enough doses. It tastes much like mint."

"You horrible woman," Aldine accused, drawing attention to her. "You've been giving me that 'mint' tea since the moment I arrived. All along you were poisoning me. Why?"

"I don't know what you're talking about. I gave you nothing I didn't have myself, did I? This is simply your mad paranoia speaking. That's all. No one has tried to kill you. No one believes you."

"And psilocybe are mushroom, producing powerful hallucinations. They can be ground up and put in anything."

"The vanilla sauce," Aldine stated. "I was the only one who had it."

"I had some too and it didn't do anything to me."

"But you didn't eat it," Weber said. "It was untouched on your plate when I cleared them away."

"Be quiet, you stupid old man. No one cares what you have to say."

"But you dumped these in the forest," Wolfgang cut in.

"Yes, why did you?" Ludwig said, turning to her.

187

"Says him. Everyone knows he's had it out for me from the first day I arrived. No point denying it," she said, turning to Wolfgang. "It is probably yours. You are the one who has caused all the problems here," Elke said with raised eyebrows as if she was making a point. "You are the jealous one. Have been all your life."

Aldine shifted as close as she could. "Why does she hate you, Wolfgang?"

Everyone turned to him. "Because she tried to seduce me and I wanted nothing to do with it. From the start she wanted to manipulate me to do her bidding, but I never played along, and her regard turned very sour after that."

Wilhelmina gasped.

"Liar!" Elke roared. Turning her attention to Ludwig, she walked closer to him. "They're lying. They're all lying. She is the crazy one and they're blaming it on me. I didn't do anything. She is the one doing this. She is mad, ran off a cliff. What was I supposed to do?" Tears were flowing down her cheeks. Deep groves of concern marred Ludwig's countenance. He wanted to believe his wife, but he had doubts.

"The scuffle marks of an altercation are quite clear from where Aldine fell," Heinrich added calmly.

Elke's tears stopped and her face turned cold before she bared her teeth and rushed for Heinrich with her fingers like claws, aiming for his face, but she wasn't strong enough against the grip he took on her wrists. "How dare you accuse me? You're the one the curse is on. You should have sent her away. Why couldn't you just do as you were supposed to? This is all your fault."

"You killed Josefina and Luise," Heinrich accused.

"You killed them," she shot back. There was no mask now, her rage was fully revealed. "You are the one the curse is on, don't you see? It was all you. So arrogant and stupid. You never understood anything. And him," she said, turning to Wolfgang, "always that raging jealousy. He would have turned on you eventually, all of you. Don't you see that? He's responsible. He just now walked into the house with those substances, didn't he? Had them all along. I won't let you blame any of this on me. He was the one who pushed that whore off the cliff. Probably'd had enough of her." Elke positively glowed with righteous indignation, masking sheer desperation.

"Elke," Ludwig warned, taking her by the waist. "He could not have. He was with me when Aldine fell—was pushed." Elke looked at him as he had conducted the deepest betrayal. "What have you done?"

She faltered for a moment. "It was all for you. Don't you see that? You deserve so much more—we deserve so much more." Everyone stood in shocked silence, until Ludwig finally picked her up and carried her from the room.

"I think we had better summon the police," Heinrich said.

"She will hang if you do," Wilhelmina said. "There will be scandal."

"She cannot stay here," Wolfgang said disbelievingly. "She murders anyone who gets in the way of her ambition."

"Which is what, exactly?" Wilhelmina asked.

"To be countess. She just admitted it. That has always been her goal."

For a second, it looked like Wilhelmina wanted to argue, but she couldn't. Elke had just admitted her reasoning. The whole house now had a shocked stillness. Where Elke had been taken, Aldine had no idea. Poor Ludwig. No one had looked as shocked and betrayed as he had.

Still carrying the pouches, Doctor Hagen came up the stairs. There was a heaviness in his step that reflected the mood everyone felt. For Aldine, it also felt as if everything had been uncovered, the festering wound hidden in this house had been revealed.

Arriving to her, the doctor sighed. "You are lucky to be alive in more ways than I thought. In large enough doses, pennyroyal poisoning can lead to paralysis and death."

"I think that is how Josefina died. She died of a fever, did she not? And she had had the same fever-ridden dreams I did."

"There is a good chance, but we will never really know." Taking the handles from Anna, he wheeled her back to her bedroom.

"I suspect she will continue to blame Wolfgang. It is her only chance."

"Then she underestimates the bond between brothers," Doctor Hagen said. "There is too much evidence against her."

"But she did drink the pennyroyal herself. I saw her on many occasions."

"Perhaps she didn't want to risk becoming pregnant until she knew her ambitions were realized—in case she needed to cut her losses. I suspect if they look into her past, they will find other evidence of her ambition."

"How could someone kill people for a title—people they sit next to every single day?"

"It would take a very twisted mind."

Heinrich appeared at the door and Doctor Hagen took his leave. Anna left the room too.

"We will have her committed," he said. "It is the best place for her. She will live out her days in an institution where she cannot harm anyone. I agree with this decision. For one, I do not wish any more blood on my hands."

"You are not responsible for any of this."

"If I hadn't so willfully ignored what was being told to me, perhaps I would have seen this—perhaps I would have stopped this from happening. Even you were almost taken from me, and throughout I struggled to believe the things you told me. I will carry that guilt for a long time."

Sitting down on the bed, he took her hand as she sat in the wheelchair. Aldine could commiserate with that guilt. She would feel the same if she had ignored such things—even as she would suspect the person making such claims were mad. It was different when one was the person going through it.

"Those mushrooms are very powerful. I literally saw and felt the world breaking into pieces, but I knew she was trying to harm me. I was just too addled to stop her. That was perhaps the point. I never wish to know those mushrooms again."

"Sadly they grow all over the forest. I will teach you which ones are safe to pick, or we will all have an interesting supper."

Aldine smiled at the thought. *God forbid.* "It is over, isn't it?"

"Yes," Heinrich said. "She will not harm anyone again. Ludwig has her locked in her room. He will take her to Switzerland tomorrow, where she will be cared for by professionals. She will never return. He is devastated."

"Poor Ludwig."

"I suspect, in time, he will seek a divorce, but I do not know. He will have to decide what to do with her, but we will not desert her completely. We don't have to leave her to the cruelty and mercy of the madhouse—instead an institution where she will be cared for. She is insane—we do not wish for her to suffer."

Aldine nodded, although she wasn't entirely convinced Elke wasn't simply evil. Treating her with kindness was perhaps the right thing to do. Heinrich was always kind and it was the reason Aldine adored him. Leaning over, he kissed her.

"I must go help with the preparations. In the morning, she will go."

Aldine nodded as he rose and left.

Taking a deep breath, she realized it truly was over. The incessant darkness that she had felt encroaching on her was over. The battle had been fought and won. The enemy had been hidden, but she was now uncovered. All this time, the misdirection and the accusation of witchcraft, the constant suspicion—it was all over.

Chapter 32

IT WAS A TENSE NIGHT, but not because of any disturbances to her peace, other than Aldine going over in her mind what had happened and the things Elke had done. They were still incomprehensible.

She was being taken away this morning. Ludwig was to drive her to Switzerland, where she was to be placed in a better institution than she deserved, because Aldine didn't think she was insane—just callous and ambitions. Evil even. The woman didn't care at all about the impact her ambition had on others. But luckily that ambition had finally been thwarted.

Out the window, Aldine heard her leave without much fanfare. They simply got into the carriage and drove off. And then the house was quiet. The evil that had dogged the house was gone.

Shortly after, steps approached her room and Heinrich appeared. "She is gone," he said. He still looked troubled by these latest events and revelations.

"Hopefully there will be peace in this house."

"I believe Ludwig intends to continue traveling after. This has all been quite a shock to him."

Was it horrible to say she was glad? He had been such a strong detractor, attacking her character and sanity. At some point he would come back, but she would have to deal with that then.

"There will be awkward questions about her whereabouts. It worries mother," he said with a note of exasperation.

Was it horrible that she wasn't overly concerned about Wilhelmina's worry about social consequences either? Although she could imagine Wilhelmina squirm when Lady Thainor asked what had happened to Elke, not that the woman had ever really cared about Elke. Aldine remembered how dismissed Elke had been by the lady. Perhaps that dismissal was what drove someone like her to murder people around her. A shudder went down Aldine's back.

"She is a bit lost for words at the moment," he continued. "She can't understand how she didn't see it."

"Elke was good at hiding herself and her intentions. I never saw it either until she pushed me off a cliff."

"You are lucky to be alive. I am so relieved you are alive. When I saw you down there, my heart sank. I was devastated. But when we got to you, you opened your eyes." Leaning over, he stroked her cheek. "It is inconceivable what she took away from me—and tried to. I am not sure I can forgive her."

"I suppose it is too much to ask for you to forget her."

"But we must be happy," he stated.

Aldine smiled. That was exactly what she wanted. "Then let's be happy."

Rising, he kissed her. "I will go build our bed," he said and left.

*

It took weeks for Aldine's leg to heal, but it finally did. Their existence was peaceful, especially since Wilhelmina had decided to visit her sister for a while. She had been quiet and introverted since Elke's proclivities had been revealed.

Now it was only the two of them in the house and for the first time, Aldine felt as if it was truly her and Heinrich together. It was a bit lonely during the days, but she loved missing him, and then he would come home and they would eat and sit in the salon and chat until it was time to go upstairs. Even the house felt peaceful. The dark decor inside didn't seem so oppressive; it was more comfortable.

Today, though, it was a nice day and Aldine felt restless. She hadn't walked much for a while and now she felt like she needed to get out of the house, so she walked along familiar paths, staying away from the cliff from where she had fallen. She wasn't ready to revisit the place and the awful, terrified feelings she'd had there.

Instead, she walked the narrowing path to that place few people ever went—to the witches' cottage. There was still a question praying on her mind. What had been real and what had been induced by the substances Elke had given her? The fever and the feelings of fire were explained by the pennyroyal, but the dreams, the betrayal, the heat—that had felt different.

Part of her accepted that it were the mad ravings of a person under the influence of mind-altering substances, but another part of her had trouble shaking the things she had seen in her dreams. It felt as if something was unanswered.

As she approached the hollow where the witches' cottage was, she saw a different place than before. It had entirely fallen down, as if whatever had been holding it up had given. There was just a jumble of mossy bumps on the ground. The witches' cottage was no more.

It wasn't them that had tried to kill her or the two women before her—that had been Elke's very real ambition. In fact, Elke had been the one talking about a curse to rear fear and worry. She had used it to generate the kind of neurotic behavior she'd wanted.

Taking a last look at the remnants of the past, she turned back. That feeling of heaviness wasn't here anymore either, but unfortunately Aldine couldn't tell what was Elke's influence and what was not. The story of the witches and what had happened to them wasn't a lie. The trials had happened and the women who had lived here had been persecuted.

She had seen that witch being burned in the painting and she would bet her life it had not been there before, and that was clearly before Elke had started feeding her those hallucination-inducing mushrooms. Their effect was never in question, and until she had seen that addition to the painting, she had never seen anything of her fears manifested. But then, it could be that Elke had painted it there when the room had been left empty.

With a deep sigh, she started to walk back the way she had come. Even the forest held no fear for her now. The last time she'd come here, the feeling of unease had been palpable—now it felt almost comforting.

Back at the house, she stopped by the workshop where their bed was almost finished. Heinrich wasn't there—instead at the mill, seeing to the work there. Wolfgang was gone. Aldine hadn't seen him in days. He ate supper with them quite often, but he rarely stayed otherwise. Heinrich suspected he had a sweetheart somewhere in the village. Aldine hoped so.

Absently, she put her hand on her belly. Her monthly had not arrived, but she didn't feel sickly like some said she would. If by next month, she still hadn't bled, then she would tell Heinrich. He would be beside himself. Children running around the house was something he dearly wanted, and how things were now, they would make a wonderful family. Hope surged in her, but she guarded herself against disappointment. In her heart, though, she knew there was a child growing inside her.

A gentle breeze rustled through the leaves and the sun shone. It really was a lovely day. Away from the house, Weber was pottering around in the herb garden. Anna was probably in the kitchen with the cook. They kept to themselves if they weren't needed, and everyone seemed happy that way.

There were no feelings of foreboding when she walked into the house. It was just a house, but something drew her attention, told her to pay attention. Drawing her back at the painting, a market scene. Nothing moved, nothing terrifying was there, but the hair on the back of her neck stood up. In the very distance was the tiny depiction of a pyre and a woman burning.

Aldine stared at it for a moment. She was sure it hadn't been there before. "I swear," she said through gritted teeth, "so much as a peep out of you and I will burn every painting in this house."

There was no response, no shift in temperature or atmosphere. No currents of heat. All was like it had been before. A clock ticked gently from the hallway. There was nothing. The small depiction just sat there as if completely forgotten and unnoticed by the townspeople in the market.

"Weber," she called and it took a moment for the man to arrive. "Do you see that?" she asked, pointing to the tiny pyre in the picture.

Looking closely, he squinted. "I never noticed that before. They were different times back then."

"Yes," Aldine said, not quite sure what to think. It had been many weeks since Elke had been taken away, but there hadn't been so much as a peep of anything untoward in the house. Nothing scary or ominous. No fiery dreams or hot currents. Everything was peaceful. Perhaps the witches just wanted to tell their story—an echo of the atrocities of the past.

Either way, Aldine would keep an eye on them and if they stepped out of line, she would act. Somehow, though, she had the feeling they had told their story to her already, and there were worse things to fear in the world than long-dead witches. "Behave," she said firmly.

The End

To find out about new releases, please sign up to my Readers' Group at www.camilleoster.com.

Other books by Camille Oster

The Curse at Rose Hill - The glittering and bright regency society of Montserrat, a Caribbean Island, exists only because of the miserable toil of some. The accepted unjustness of it jars Miss Emmeline Durrant who arrives from Boston to be a companion to a Mrs. Thornton, but being alone in the world, it is an opportunity she cannot afford to pass up. Even so, her welcome proves less than earnest and secrets emerge from every shadowed corner as she takes up her new position at the Rose Hill plantation.

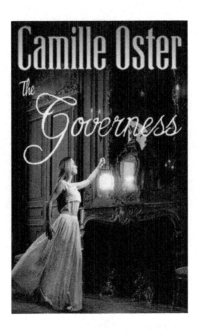

The Governess - Traveling beyond England hadn't come into Estelle Winstone's mind when she received a response to her advertisement for a position as governess. That she would have to travel all the way to Hungary sent nerves twisting inside her gut, as would meeting the mysterious count who would now be her employer. Unable to speak the language or with much to guide her, she found her new home nestled in remote mountains where hungry wolves prowled outside a dark and drafty castle scared by a long history and recent tragedies.

The Discarded Wife - Victorian London is a cruel place for a divorcee, but with the death of Sophie Duthie's beloved second husband, she is now a widow, and independent for the first time in her life. She might not have much in terms of means, but with the help of her music shop, she can support herself and her son, Alfie. Even though her second marriage was happy, Sophie is done with husbands. Her first marriage taught her well that fairy tales are nothing more than illusions.

Printed in Great Britain
by Amazon

18754984R00119